Happy Reading!

Gloria Morgan

Kinmer was a Norman knight who fought for William the Conqueror at the Battle of Hastings in 1066 and was rewarded with a lea of land.

It's twenty years later and the Saxon villagers of Kinmers Lea are in revolt against King William's 'Doomsday' taxation.

12-year-old Edwin overhears a plot against the Lord of the Manor. Can he and his Gran stop the plotters or are they too late?

Edwin and his Gran know things that nobody else around them could possibly know. Will that help or hinder them in their quest?

*An imaginative tale, well told, packed with fun!*

*Historical Novels Review*

Gloria Morgan has been writing since she was ten. She grew up in London but now lives half way up the M1, on the left. Her favourite colour is red and her favourite day is Thursday. She's had various jobs in offices, colleges, hospitals and photographic studios while the stories and plays have just kept coming. She enjoys travelling and some of the interesting people and places she's seen have found their way into her books. Best of all, Gloria likes to write for young readers. When she's not working at her computer she enjoys pottering in her garden and going for long walks, preferably with a dog. To find out about her latest project visit her website: www.gloriamorgan.co.uk

# Kinmers Lea

## GLORIA MORGAN

An environmentally friendly book printed and bound in
England by www.printondemand-worldwide.com

 **Mixed Sources**
Product group from well-managed
forests, and other controlled sources
www.fsc.org Cert no. TT-COC-002641
© 1996 Forest Stewardship Council

PEFC Certified
This product is
from sustainably
managed forests
and controlled
sources
www.pefc.org
PEFC/16-33-415

This book is made entirely of chain-of-custody materials

A CIP catalogue record for this title is available
from the British Library

ISBN
978-178035-442-2

First published in 2008
Second Edition 2012
by
Callie-Co Books, Nottingham

www.callie-cobooks.co.uk

# Kinmers Lea

# CHAPTER 1

"Mum, can't I stop at home while you go?"

"Don't be silly, Edwin. You're only twelve. You can't possibly stay here by yourself."

No surprises there. He wasn't allowed to do anything by himself.

Mum was determined he was going with her to visit one of her old school friends in the north of England. It was a totally stupid idea. He'd never even seen the woman. He'd been trying to think of a way out of going ever since Mum mentioned it, but she wouldn't budge. He had to go. What a way to end the summer holidays.

On their journey up from Winchester he'd started seriously wondering if he could escape when they stopped at the motorway services. No chance.

It just hadn't occurred to him that breaking their journey at Granny's would solve his problem. He'd never met Granny before today. He certainly hadn't expected her to invite him to stop over.

When his Mum's car pulled up outside Granny's door he had been so dreading it. Mum had told him his great-grandmother was ninety. Whatever was she going to be like?

He couldn't believe it when Granny came walking out briskly to greet them. She was not much taller than Edwin himself. Her grey hair was drawn back from her face into a bun at the nape of her neck. She was wearing long, old-fashioned clothes. He had to look twice when he noticed a pair of very modern trainers peeping out from under her skirt.

She ushered them into the cottage, which smelled of polish and freshly baked scones.

"Come in. Come in. I've just made a pot of tea."

Granny had flashed him a smile as she followed Mum through to the sitting room with a tea tray.

"Your tea's on the draining board, Edwin. Help yourself to scones. Jam and cream on the table. See you later."

The door closed behind her leaving Edwin alone in the kitchen.

He couldn't believe it. Edwin didn't often hug people but he really felt he could have made an exception then.

His mug of tea stood steaming on a scrubbed wooden draining board attached to a deep stone sink with big brass taps. Everything in the kitchen was very old fashioned but spotlessly clean. A big black cooker took up most of the wall opposite the sink. He could feel the warmth coming out of it and a smell of cooking too.

He took his tea to the table, intending to sit down, but there were no chairs. There was a big plate full of scones. He picked one and stood and served himself with jam and cream. It was so good he had another. And then, after that, a third.

When Granny came back into the kitchen she had a surprise for him:

"I've had a word with your Mum. You don't have to go visiting with her if you don't want to. You can stop here with me, if you'd rather."

Edwin wiped the crumbs from his mouth. He couldn't believe Mum had agreed. Better fetch his back-pack in from the car quickly before she changed her mind.

"Your mother's worried you might find Nottinghamshire boring."

Edwin shrugged. Well, yeah. He might be dead bored here or he might not. Anything was better than being dragged along on this trip with Mum.

"You'll be in the room on the right at the top of the stairs. And don't bother bringing anything in that you need to plug in because there's no electricity upstairs."

That might be a problem. He wondered what the fault was and how soon it could be fixed.

It was a bit odd to think he would be on his own with a complete stranger for a few days.

Only standing together at the front gate, waving Mum on her way, Granny didn't feel like a stranger.

"I hope your Mum enjoys her visiting. Who is it she's going to stay with?"

"I haven't got a clue!"

They both laughed out loud.

Granny reached up and picked a hard little apple from a tree near the gate. She polished it on her sleeve and held it out. Although it didn't look very nice, Edwin took it and tried a small bite. He was amazed how juicy and tasty it was. He quickly munched the whole of it, right down to the core.

"You ever been scrumping?" Granny wanted to know.

"What's that?"

"Evidently not. Scrumping is climbing over walls and pinching apples off other people's trees, without getting caught."

Edwin smiled. He didn't think Mum would approve of that.

"What vegetables are we going to have for supper?" Granny wondered.

The green leaves growing in the dirt at their feet all looked the same to Edwin. He didn't fancy eating any of them.

Granny bent down and pulled up a carrot. She removed the top leaves with a twist of her wrist, wiped off some bits of earth on her apron and handed it to Edwin.

"Have a bite."

"What, just like it is?"

"Why not? You ate the apple off the tree. What's the difference? Try it."

Edwin couldn't see any way out. He took a half-hearted bite at the carrot and couldn't believe how sweet and crunchy it was. He ate it all.

"Carrots for supper, then, Edwin. And we'll have some runner beans to go with them."

Granny led the way to a row of tall wooden poles with plants growing up them. She pulled off some long thin green things that were hanging down among the leaves.

Then she fetched a spade and showed Edwin how to dig up potatoes. She lifted the hem of her long apron and held it out to make a carrier for the vegetables.

"Do you like gooseberries?"

"I don't know."

Granny pointed to some bushes on the opposite side of the garden.

"Over there. Pick as many as you can. Be careful. They've got wicked thorns on them."

Granny wasn't exaggerating. There were huge spikes sticking out of the stems. Between the thorns, Edwin could see fat green fruits tinged with red. He managed to get twenty.

"Will this be enough?" He carried them into the kitchen in the front of his tee shirt, holding it up like Granny had held her apron.

"Perfect. I'll make a crumble.

Gran set Edwin to fetching dishes from the big walk-in larder while she mixed up ingredients in a bowl and made the crumble.

"We need some logs, Edwin. Go out of the back door and round to your left and bring me as many as you can carry off the pile."

Edwin did as he was told, wondering what Granny was going to do with them. Surely she didn't have a recipe for logs?

Granny made Edwin stand back from the cooker, then opened one of its numerous doors. An unexpected blast of heat came out and nearly scorched him. He could see a glowing fire inside touched with silvery ash. Sparks flew as Granny pushed in the logs he had fetched and closed the door.

Edwin stood rigid. At home they had an electric stove. This was something else.

Further along the front of the cooker Granny opened another door that belonged to an oven. She popped the crumble in.

When they were nearly ready to eat, Granny got out a bottle of elderflower cordial and poured them each a drink.

"Wash your hands before you have your dinner, Edwin."

"Er, Granny . . . Where's the toilet?"

"Outside, on the left, past the wood pile. You'll have to come back into the kitchen to wash your hands."

Edwin ventured outside to the loo and was very glad to find it was a flush toilet. When he pulled the long chain hanging down from a metal box in the roof, there was a satisfactory swoosh of water. Edwin wondered what would happen if he needed the loo in the night. He was glad it wasn't the middle of winter.

He came back in to wash his hands. Granny appeared to have read his mind.

"No need to go out in the middle of the night. You'll find a chamber pot under the bed in your room so you don't have to venture outside in the dark."

"Er . . . thanks, Gran."

Edwin wondered what else he would have to get used to, staying in the country.

Granny's chicken casserole with dumplings and vegetables followed by her gooseberry crumble tasted better than any meal Edwin could remember. He cleared his plate. He helped Granny wash and dry the dishes.

"Gran, can I go outside and have a walk round the back garden?"

"Of course you can. It's nearly dark so mind how you go."

Edwin let himself out of the back door and stood for a moment while his eyes got accustomed to the fading light.

Here, everything was allowed to grow in its own way. All kinds of flowers were blooming. Climbing plants scrambled up every fence and almost covered several small out-buildings.

As he wandered round, Edwin decided he really liked this place a lot. He couldn't remember when he'd felt so happy and relaxed.

When he went back into the cottage he found Gran comfortably settled in the sitting room, a book open on her knee. The room was bathed in a soft, orange light from a big brass lamp on the mantelpiece.

"What's in those little buildings all covered with plants?"

"I use them for storing garden tools, but in times past people used to keep chickens in them, even pigs."

"Really?"

"Yes. There's a well in the garden, too, but that was covered over a long time ago."

"Is this place really old, then?"

"It is. And I expect there were other houses here long before this particular one was built."

"How long have you lived here, Gran?"

"All my life."

"Gran . . . Are you really my great-grandmother?"

"I am."

"Mum said you're ninety."

"Did she? What do you think about that?"

Edwin thought being ninety was gross. He stared down at his socks. He had a strange feeling Granny could read his mind.

"I expect you imagined I'd be totally gaga, sitting propped up, with some person in a plastic apron spooning soup into me?"

"That's horrible, Gran."

"I know. People as old as me shouldn't be allowed."

Edwin dared to glance up. Sharp blue eyes were watching him. Granny smiled and they both burst out laughing.

"Tell me some more about the cottage, Gran."

"I was born here. The house been in our family for generations. And I'm sure it will stay in the family for generations to come. Very little has changed over the years, apart from the plumbing. When I was a little girl I used to think about all the people who've lived here before me, wondered what they were like, what they did, whether they were happy or sad."

Edwin looked round the room.

"Granny, where is your telly?"

"I haven't got one."

"What? You don't have a telly?"

"No."

Edwin's glance fell on the lamp. Granny read his thoughts again.

"It's an oil lamp."

"You said something about there's no electricity in the bedrooms . . ."

"That's right. There's no electricity downstairs either. You can take a candle up to bed. There's a night-light candle on the dressing table that will burn all night, in case you're nervous of the dark. We don't have street lights in the country, you know."

Edwin took his lighted candle upstairs to get undressed. He liked the simple, painted bedroom furniture – a chair, a small chest of drawers, a mirror on the wall, a bedside table.

He got down on his knees and inspected the pink and white china chamber pot under the bed. It was like a giant tea cup. Maybe everybody who lived in the country made use of one, but Edwin vowed he would have to be on the point of death before he used his. It was just too gross.

He came downstairs in his pyjamas and braved the darkness outside the backdoor to pay a last minute call while Granny made cocoa. Then he went up to bed.

"Sleep tight, Edwin."

It was a warm night and the flower-scented air wafted in through the open window. He decided not to bother with the night-light.

Crossing his fingers that he could last until morning without needing the loo again, he blew out his candle and settled down to sleep in the solid black darkness of the countryside night.

# CHAPTER 2

Edwin was woken in the middle of the night by the sound of Granny calling his name. He had no idea what time it was. Outside it was pitch black.

He sat up, listening intently. He could hear footsteps going down the stairs and then the front door opened. What was the matter with Gran? Why had she called out to him? Something must be wrong. He'd better go after her.

Edwin quickly slipped out of bed. He felt around for the chair where he had put his clothes when he got undressed and hastily put them on again – long khaki shorts that came half way down his calves and a brown tee shirt with a big splashy pattern in white on the front. He pulled on his khaki socks that matched his shorts and wriggled his feet into his trainers.

He hesitated for a moment and then picked up his black fleece hoodie. Okay, it was summer time, but it might be chilly outside in the night. He tied the sleeves round his waist. Then he felt his way carefully to the door, so he didn't graze his shins on the furniture, let himself out and followed Granny down the stairs.

When he got to the bottom the front door was wide open. He followed her out into the garden but couldn't see her anywhere. He spotted a slight movement to the right side of the house. Just as he was about to call out to her, there was a gust of wind and the front door slammed shut behind him. It made him jump. He just had to hope Granny had her key with her, otherwise they were locked out.

"Gran? Where are you?"

No answer. She must have gone round to the back.

The first thing was to find her and make sure she was all right.

Edwin moved across to the right side of the house, where the runner beans grew. Funny, he didn't remember them being so overgrown yesterday. But now, as he struggled in the dark, he couldn't find a way past them. They grew like a solid barrier across the path round to the back garden.

He turned away and crossed over to the other side of the house. The path went all the way round so he would go that way. Except when he got to the left side, the fruit bushes seemed to have doubled and trebled in size since he was there picking gooseberries for supper. There was an impenetrable thorn hedge there now, taller than himself and as sharp as barbed wire.

He backed away again and returned to the front door. When he tried it, it was definitely locked. It felt strange under his fingers. More rough and grainy than before. He peered at it. It looked different. His eyes must be playing tricks with him. He wasn't used to trying to see things with next to no light.

There was no moon and the few stars that were not obscured by clouds seemed very small and distant. It was a warm night but there was a breeze blowing and it was carrying a very distinctive countryside smell. The local farmer must have done some muck spreading after Edwin had gone to bed last night.

Edwin went back to the bean row. However difficult it was to get through, it would be easier than battling with the thorn bushes. He pushed his way forward. These beans were not going to stop him getting round to the back. They were vegetables, for god's sake! He kicked at the lower leaves with his feet and then threw himself with all his might against the intertwining stems and stalks.

For a long moment he hung there, like a fly caught in a web, and then quite suddenly the plants seemed to wilt under his weight and he was able to scramble through.

When he was on the other side he shook himself and brushed a few leaf bits out of his hair. Well, that was something to tell Granny. She'd better get her runner beans back under control. Stop putting fertiliser on them.

Edwin picked his way carefully round to the back of the house and looked about for Granny. She couldn't be far away, surely.

He tried to get his bearings. Everything seemed so changed in the dark. He heard a slight noise and headed off towards it.

To his relief, beyond a couple of bushes and an untidy pile of straw, which he didn't recollect seeing earlier, there was Granny, crouched down and apparently listening hard. He hurried forward.

"Shhh!" She held up a finger to her lips and he immediately stopped still. Then she beckoned him forward with a finger. As soon as he got near enough she grabbed the end of one of the sleeves tied round his waist and whispered urgently to him:

"Mind how you go, Edwin!"

Because Gran was whispering, Edwin whispered back.

"Why? What's the matter, Gran?"

"That hole in the ground just by your right foot is the well, and if you fall in, there's no way anybody's going to be able to get you out."

Edwin backed away as fast as he could. Using the sleeve of his fleece, Granny reeled him in towards her until he was crouching down at her side.

"What are we doing Gran?"

"Look at the house."

"What about it?"

"Well, what does it look like to you?"

Edwin peered closely through the branches of the bush. The house bore no resemblance at all to Granny's neat and tidy cottage. Where, in daylight, the windows had gleamed with frequent polishing, now there were only rough, open holes without glass, with sacking hung across them. No appetising smell of cooking came from the kitchen. Instead, the whole yard smelled like a very neglected toilet.

He could hear the murmur of voices from inside the house.

"What's going on, Gran? Where are we?"

"We're in my garden, or so I believe. As to what's going on, that's what I'm trying to find out."

"But if this is your garden, that ought to be your house, only it isn't."

"Correct, Edwin. I think it's not so much a question of 'where are we?' as 'when are we?'"

"I don't understand."

"We know the place we're in, but not the year."

"Your house, but ages and ages ago?"

"Correct again, Edwin."

"So who's inside your house?"

"I don't know. Let's listen and see what we can pick up from their conversation."

A voice speaking near the window opening carried to their hiding place.

"So that's my plan," a man was saying. "What do you think of it?"

There was a moment's hesitation before another voice replied:

"Well, it's a great idea, Stan, but do you think we can carry it off? I mean to say, she'll be pretty well guarded, won't she?"

"That's where Bebba comes in. She's got herself taken on as nurse-maid and she's going to let me know when the coast is clear. As soon as you get my signal, Wiglaf and Fred, you two go in and grab her. You put a sack over her head and another over her feet, roll her up in a rug and carry her out on your shoulders. Bebba says there's people going about the camp all the time, carrying gear like that. Nobody will question you.

"Bebba will bring the baby. People are used to seeing her carrying him about so she won't be stopped. We'll have Arnie and Garth waiting, in position, on a cart with horses – I know, I know, Garth, but horses are quicker than oxen – and we'll have them away from there and hidden beyond any man's sight before the alarm's given."

Edwin's eyes grew rounder and rounder as he listened. He couldn't believe his ears.

"Gran . . ."

"Shhh!" The finger went to the lips again and he fell silent. He didn't know how to contain all the questions that were flying round in his brain.

Another voice joined in the conversation, louder and more strident than the others:

"It'll serve him right. We don't want him here, taking what's ours, lording it over us, giving us orders, treating us like slaves. My father and my father's father worked this land as freemen and here I stand, no better than a serf. Let's give him something to take his mind off counting us and taxing us and taking away our freedom!"

The other voices joined in a general mutter of agreement.

There was a pause and then Edwin heard gulping noises. He guessed they were drinking to the success of their plan.

But what a plan! It sounded as if they were plotting a kidnapping. He simply had to talk to Gran and see if she had understood the same as he had.

He nudged her and used sign language to tell her that he wanted them to move away so they could speak. Gran nodded but kept crouched low as she led him carefully round the open hole in the ground that was the well, skirting the muddy ground at its edges, and back towards the bean row.

"Gran, did you hear what I heard? They're going to kidnap some lady, aren't they? And a baby. Who is she? What are they going to do to her?"

"I think you're right Edwin. Kidnapping is in the air. It seems the local residents have a grudge against somebody and want to punish him by snatching his wife and child."

"But that's terrible, Gran. They shouldn't do that. What sort of people are they?"

"Well, that depends. You could describe them as a terrorist cell. Or you could say they're a band of freedom fighters."

"What do you mean, Gran? What's the difference?"

"The only difference, Edwin, is what side you happen to be on yourself."

# CHAPTER 3

Gran and Edwin crept back to their vantage point but the men indoors had moved away from the window and although they could still hear the murmur of voices they could no longer catch what was being said.

"This is no good, Edwin. We need to get closer. Hear more details of their plot."

"What shall we do, Gran?"

"What we need to do first is reconnoitre."

"What's that?"

"Take a good look round. We need to get inside without the people in there knowing."

"How can we do that?"

"Trust me, Edwin. I was with the Commando's in World War Two. I learned all the tricks of the trade.

If you think this lot is good at plotting, you haven't seen me in action."

Granny dropped to her hands and knees.

"If you hear anything creaking, that'll be my joints, Edwin. You wait here."

With that, Granny started to crawl towards the rear part of the cottage, looking back over her shoulder every now and then to make sure she hadn't been spotted.

There was a long, low addition at the back, at right angles to the main part of the building. Although the window openings there were smaller, they were nearer the ground.

Granny straightened up and peered into each one in turn and at the last one she turned back and beckoned to Edwin as she hitched up her skirts.

He crouched down low and crept to her side.

Granny held her finger up to her lips again and kept her voice to a whisper.

"I think we'll be all right here, Edwin. Give me a leg up."

Edwin cupped his hands to make a foot-hold. He gave a good heave to give Granny a lift and realised, too late, that he'd heaved too hard. Granny did a perfect cart-wheel through the window, her skirt and apron flying up over her head.

Edwin couldn't help seeing a pair of thick, baggy, grey woollen pantaloons, with a row of pockets down each leg, buttoned down over her socks below Granny's skinny knees.

Next moment Granny had picked herself up and dusted herself down. Edwin was very relieved to see she seemed unhurt.

"You all right, Gran?"

"Shhh! I'm fine, thank you, Edwin. I saw you admiring my bloomers."

Edwin blushed scarlet at the thought that Granny had noticed him noticing her underwear.

"I inherited them from a great-aunt who had them from Amelia Bloomer herself."

"Who's she?"

"Amelia Bloomer was the first woman ever to ride a bicycle in public. Women's fashions then were long, tight skirts down to the floor. You can't get far on a bike wearing one of those, so Amelia Bloomer invented sportswear. The most useful article of clothing I've ever owned. I'm glad you approve of them."

Granny reached out a hand to him through the window gap. Her grip, when he took her hand, was like a vice. Edwin scrambled up the wall and launched himself into a straw-filled space that was even more smelly than the yard outside.

"Pooh! What's that pong?"

Granny pointed.

"Bit whiffy, I agree."

Edwin straightened up and found himself looking at the backside of a large brown cow. Only on closer inspection it wasn't a cow, it was more like a bull.

"What . . . ?"

"Ox. Won't hurt you. Docile like a cow but bigger, stronger and smellier."

Nevertheless, Edwin took a step back. The ox was massive and it had the biggest pair of pointed horns curving up from its head. It only had to rub itself up against the wall to scratch an itch, and Edwin would be a smear on the woodwork.

Edwin was not a natural with animals. He'd never even had a hamster. He would have preferred much more space between himself and this mountain on four legs.

Granny squeezed past the beast. Edwin held his breath when she gave it a good smack on the rump but it only twitched its ears and carried on chewing.

"Aren't you scared of it, Granny? It's so big . . . "

"No. I was in the Land Army during the war. Got used to cattle, horses, dogs, all sorts. You've just got to let them know who's boss."

"I thought you said you were in the Commando's."

"The war went on a long time, Edwin. I got about a bit. Saw life. All good experience."

Edwin followed Granny as they squeezed their way along a row of stalls which contained another ox and several cows. The air was thick with the animals' heavy breath and the reek of their droppings in the damp straw. Edwin was convinced he was going to pass out at any minute. He staggered from one window opening to the next, taking a gulp of air at every opportunity.

"How can anyone stand the smell?"

"The people who live here don't notice it. Their world is quiet on the ears but loud on the nose. In our century we live with all kinds of noise these people wouldn't be able to tolerate, like they accept the stink that we can't bear."

Edwin went along behind Granny, still gasping, until they reached the point where the animals' shed joined on to the house. Granny stopped at the foot of a rough wooden ladder that led up to an opening in the ceiling.

"This is where we're going. Don't you set foot on the ladder until I'm up in case it won't take the weight of two. I'm guessing the floor up there will be the ceiling of the room where the men were talking. We should be able to hear every word."

Granny put her foot on the first rung, then turned and added:

"Just remember, they'll be able to hear every sound we make too, so don't sneeze out loud."

Edwin waited at the foot of the ladder. Granny signalled down to him to follow her and he quickly climbed up. The loft space at the top was dark apart from a few bars of dull candle light that shone through the gaps between the floorboards. At least it didn't smell as bad as the shed. There were bundles of hay and bits of wood and leather scattered about.

"Stay here and make sure you don't knock anything over," Granny whispered.

Granny lay down flat on her stomach and edged her way across the floor, propelling herself an inch at a time by the toes of her trainers.

What seemed like a long time later, Edwin heard her hiss softly to him. He got down flat and manoeuvred himself carefully along until he was beside Granny.

All Edwin could see below, through the narrow cracks in the boards, was a great deal of hair, none of it too clean. He counted five men. As well as the long, untidy hair on their heads, all the men had big bushy beards and moustaches.

One man was particularly tall and broad. He had dark, coppery red hair. He seemed to be in charge of things.

Two would probably be blond, if they ever had a shampoo. One of them was tall and broad, the other shorter and thinner. They were both taking an active part in the discussion.

Two short, stocky, sandy haired men didn't have much to say but they were listening carefully.

Edwin wondered how he would recognise any of them again, except by the tops of their heads.

He felt Gran's bony finger poke him in the ribs. He looked round, peering in the gloom, and saw her holding up a finger to her lips. He nodded to show he understood. Silence.

The red-headed man was speaking to the tall blond man. Edwin recognised his voice. It was Stan.

"I agree with you, Wiglaf. We've been used to being our own masters and none of us takes well to being demoted to servants of some foreigner."

"They can give any reason they like," the shorter blond man chipped in, "we know this survey isn't of any benefit to us."

Stan turned to him.

"That's true, enough, Fred."

"It's only to see how much they can tax us. When they've counted all our land and all our beasts, they'll send the figures down to the king in Winchester and he'll consider himself a wealthy man on the strength of what we own."

At the mention of Winchester, Edwin nearly spluttered. That was where he lived. He had to put a hand over his mouth to keep himself from making any noise. He listened even harder.

"Used to own, more like." It was the tall blond man again. "More and more of us are having our holdings confiscated. If that Grimkettle has had any hand in me losing my lands, it will be the worst for him."

"Oh, come along now, Wiglaf. He swears he was picked out at random and had no choice but to testify. He was threatened with dire punishment if he didn't. Grimkettle is a Saxon through and through. He's no lover of Lord Peverell or any of his Norman underlings."

"Peverell's the one we should aim for," Wiglaf growled. "I'd like to hatch a plot to bring him down."

Stan's head whipped round.

"It's too dangerous, Wiglaf. Too much risk. You know that Peverell's King William's own son. He's above our ambitions."

Stan would not let the conversation move in that direction. He seemed to be chairing the meeting.

"Let's settle for going after Kinmer, then." Wiglaf boomed. "He's lord of our manor so he's our rightful target."

It was Granny's turn to force herself to keep silent. Edwin could feel her wriggling with excitement beside him. She had heard something that was significant, that much was clear. He desperately wanted to know what, but he had to wait.

"So are we agreed to use Stan's plan?" It was the short blond man speaking again.

"I certainly am, Fred," Wiglaf answered. "Are you?"

"I am, at that," Fred nodded.

Stan spoke again.

"All that are in agreement, place your hand here upon the table in turn, each man's hand upon the others. Let that be a bond we make to act together."

Wiglaf moved forward.

"I'll be the first to commit to it."

Edwin heard the sound of his hand being placed down hard on a table top.

"I, Wiglaf, pledge to act with you all. What about you, Fred?"

The sound of another hand slapped against the first.

"I, Radfred, pledge the same. Come on, Arnie."

One of the sandy haired men who had so far not spoken, came forward from his corner and joined the others.

"I, Arnulf, pledge also. Come on, Garth."

The other sandy man moved to the table.

"I, Garth, likewise pledge."

Stan was the last to come forward. He made a very dramatic show of placing his hand on top of all the others.

"I, Athelstan, pledge with you all. I'm proud to stand with you, boys. Until tomorrow night, then!"

"Aye!"

"Aye!"

"Aye!"

"Aye!"

They lifted their hands from the table. Stan made a fist and shook it in the air. All the others did the same. Their voices rose in a defiant rumble.

Stan moved from one to the other, clapping them all on the shoulder.

That seemed to conclude the meeting. They moved away from the table, everyone muttering 'goodnight'.

The two sandy haired men stood at the door and saw the others out, then came back into the room. They pottered about for a bit, saying very little. Finally they both wrapped themselves up in blankets, blew out the candles and settled down to sleep on the dirt floor.

For what seemed like ages, Granny didn't move at all. Then she eased herself over on to her side and whispered:

"We might as well do the same. No-one's going to provide us with any better lodgings and I want to be here when they wake up. Goodnight, Edwin."

"Goodnight, Gran."

Edwin couldn't believe he could possibly sleep. So much had happened in such a short time, he was struggling to grasp it all. What he had just overheard whirled round and round in his head. There was so much he wanted to say to Gran, such a lot of questions he needed to ask. But while they were in the loft they couldn't speak. If they didn't stay silent, they would be discovered.

The loft was stuffy but warm. Granny was asleep beside him. There was no sound from the two sleeping men below. In spite of everything, Edwin's eyelids started to droop and in moments he fell asleep just where he lay.

# CHAPTER 4

Edwin jerked awake at the sound of loud pounding on the door of the cottage. He had no idea where he was or why he felt so uncomfortable. It was a moment before he could make sense of his surroundings. Before he could move or make a noise, Granny's firm grip on his wrist warned him to keep still and silent.

The two men downstairs had been disturbed from sleep, too. They began unwrapping themselves from their blankets. One fumbled to light a candle while the other stood up and moved towards the door.

Meanwhile, the banging continued and a loud voice called:

"Open up, in the name of King William."

The sandy haired men started moving faster. The candle bloomed into light as one of the men swung the door open.

Two tall men in chain mail pushed past him into the room. They were carrying long spears and had to duck down to get through the low doorway. When they stood up straight again inside the room, the points on the tops of their helmets were so close to the ceiling that Edwin could have reached down and touched them.

"We have come for Athelstan of Cottesale. Is he here?"

"No."

"No."

The sandy haired men huddled together, unable to take their eyes off the sharp points of the soldiers' spears.

"But he has been here. We were told he was here last night. So where is he now?"

"He left before we went to bed."

"I saw him out of the door myself."

"Did you now? And which way did he go?"

"Down the hill."

"Did he say where he was going?"

"No."

"I took it he was going home. It was late. Where else would he go?"

One of the soldiers suddenly leaned forward. With his left hand he grabbed the man who was speaking by the front of his shirt. Edwin drew back as he saw the glint of a blade in the soldier's right hand. He held a dagger up to the face of his shivering victim.

"Athelstan of Cottesale is not at his home. We've been there and given it a thorough search. A very thorough search. We'll do the same here if you don't tell us the truth. We believe he's hiding somewhere about this place."

"No!"

"No, he's not!"

"He went off before we settled down for the night."

"We'll see about that. Now, let's see what you've got in this hovel that might make a good hiding place for a man who's up to no good."

The soldier threw the cowering man away from him and Edwin saw the sandy haired man lift a hand to his face and wipe away a smear of blood.

Edwin turned to Granny in dismay.

If the place was going to be searched, they would be found, for sure. And the soldiers would be no more gentle with them.

"Shouldn't we get out?" he whispered.

"You're absolutely right, Edwin. Now's the time to leave."

Downstairs the soldiers were systematically turning over everything in the room, poking into anything that could possibly be a hiding place, looking underneath the table, feeling among the blankets.

Granny started to squirm her way backwards across the floor towards the opening with the ladder, making no noise. Edwin followed suit, desperately trying not to knock anything over in his haste.

Granny reached the ladder, ignored the rungs, put her feet on the outside rails and slid down. Edwin was not far behind, grateful that it was not a long drop to the floor. A sacking curtain that served as a door was moving slightly in the night air. Granny pushed Edwin through, into the garden. It was a relief to Edwin not having to go past the smelly oxen again.

"Won't be a second. Catch you up."

Granny disappeared back towards the loft ladder.

Edwin looked round. There was just a faint light in the sky, although it was not yet dawn. He flattened himself against the wall and hoped no-one was looking out of the cottage window. A few moments later Granny joined him and they crept away through the garden.

Edwin spotted the pile of hay by the well.

"Couldn't we hide in there?"

"Too obvious. First place they'll look. They'll jab their spears into any heap of hay or straw they see. Fancy that, do you?"

Edwin didn't and hastily glanced around for another hiding place. He couldn't see anywhere that wouldn't be obvious to the searchers. There was a hen coop that would be big enough to take cover in, but the soldiers would be sure to look in there. What were they going to do?

He could hear the search progressing in the house. One of the soldiers spoke:

"It's about time we had a look up in your loft. What have you got up there?"

"Nothing."

"Honestly, nothing at all."

"Nobody has been up there for a long time."

"We don't use it much."

As the sandy haired men continued to protest, Granny led the way towards the furthest end of the low building where the animals were housed and round the corner at the back.

"I shall need a leg up again, Edwin, only this time don't be quite so forceful. And don't make any noise."

"All right, Gran. Where are we going?"

"On the roof."

Edwin looked up. The roof seemed to be made of some sort of flimsy straw matting. He wasn't at all sure it would take their weight.

"Will it hold us? It doesn't look very strong."

"Don't worry. Put your feet exactly where I put mine. I'll go one step at a time. As soon as I'm safely up I'll reach down and give you a lift. All right?"

"All right, Gran."

"And remember, we may be out of sight, but not out of hearing. So keep quiet."

It turned out to be an easier climb up the wooden wall than Edwin had expected. Everything was built so roughly that there were plenty of footholds. Soon he was up level with Gran where the slope of the roof started. He realised that the matting was hung over the top of sturdy wooden beams. If they made sure they were standing on those, they could cling there out of sight of anyone in the garden.

"You comfortable?"

"Yes, Gran."

"Then hang on and keep quiet."

"Gran . . ."

"I said keep the volume down, Edwin."

"Sorry. I know they can't see us here from the garden. But what if they go round the other side of the building? They'll see us from there."

"I don't think they'll bother to do that, Edwin. I rather think they'll have something else on their minds."

At that moment there was a loud crash and raised voices shouting and cursing.

"What was that, Gran?"

"Sounds to me like someone fell down the loft ladder."

"Gran?"

"Yes, Edwin?"

"Why do you think that?"

"I spotted a big knot in the wood on one of the rungs about half way down. It must have fallen out and weakened the rung."

"Gran! I don't believe you."

"No. Well, I sawed through the rung actually. Not all the way through. I left just enough to take someone's weight going up but not coming back down again."

"Where did you get a saw?"

"Swiss Army knife. I never go anywhere without it. It's got a very good saw attachment. I use it for pruning the roses."

"I haven't seen you with a Swiss Army knife. Where is it? Show me."

Granny balanced precariously on one foot, hitched up her skirt and unbuttoned one of the pockets in her bloomers. She fished out a fat red pocket knife and started flicking it open. It bristled with blades, saws, corkscrews, scissors, gouges, and other odd shaped bits of metal that Edwin didn't recognise.

"Gran, you could do some serious damage with that."

"Yes. I hope so."

The soldiers staggered out into the yard, grumbling loudly.

"My helmet's jammed right over my eyes. Help me get it off! I can't budge it!"

The other soldier was yelling, obviously hurt.

"Oooow! Ouch!"

Edwin wished he could see what was going on.

"I'm the commanding officer here. I gave you an order! Come and help me get this thing off my head so I can see where I'm going!"

"Yes, sir!"

Edwin could hear them blundering round the yard, heaving and tugging at the helmet. He wondered, hopefully, if they were close enough to the open well to fall in.

"Be careful! That was my ears, you fool!"

"Sorry, sir!"

At last, however, it seemed they managed to remove the helmet.

"Look, the point's all bent! I can't go back to base with my helmet looking like that. I'd be a laughing stock. And what's the matter with you?"

"You know I was coming down the ladder behind you, sir?"

"Yes."

"When the ladder gave way and we fell down, sir?"

"Yes, and you landed right on top of me!"

"Well, it's my. . . it's my. . . it's my . . . Something seems to have stuck in me, sir. It doesn't half hurt, sir."

"It'll hurt a lot more if you don't get the spike on my helmet straightened out by the time we get back to base."

"Yes, sir."

"Here! You two! We're off now, but we'll be back. Meanwhile, you get that ladder fixed."

"Yes. We will."

"We will."

"I'll just check this pile of hay with my spear before we go."

Edwin heard the soldier poke about in the hay, and was glad he'd taken Granny's advice.

Shortly after that there were sounds of the soldiers leaving and the sandy haired men going back into the house. Granny and Edwin climbed down off the roof and sneaked back through the garden.

"Now would be a good time for you to go and hide in that pile of hay, Edwin. You'd be near enough the house to hear what the people inside are talking about."

"Okay, Gran. What are you going to do?"

"Me? I'm going to organise breakfast."

# CHAPTER 5

Edwin burrowed through the pile of hay to the side nearest the house. He found a big solid clump that held his weight and settled himself down on it. From where he sat he could observe the two men quite clearly.

He had no idea where Granny had gone. He couldn't imagine there were many opportunities for take-away breakfasts in the vicinity. However, if Granny had said she was going to organise breakfast then it was pretty certain to happen.

The voices in the house rose and fell as one or other of the men came near the window opening. They must be pacing about in the room. By the tone of their voices their discussion was very important and urgent.

"In that case, we should set out right away."

"But Stan wanted us to take horses. Where am I supposed to get horses from? He was going to organise that."

"We'll have to make do with the oxen, then."

"Well, that's a relief to me, if we do that. But I don't think Stan's going to be best pleased when he sees them."

"It'll be up to him to find an alternative then, won't it?"

"But we don't know where he is."

"We know he didn't go home last night. I reckon he got wind of the soldiers going to his place. I bet he set off to the camp there and then."

"But we said tonight, Arnie."

"I know. But what would you do in the circumstances? He can't go home, so it would make sense to bring the mission forward."

"But that's not what we agreed."

"Ten-to-one he expects us to work it out for ourselves that there's been a change of plan. I say we should set off right now. If I know Stan, he'll be keeping an eye out for us and he'll met us there."

"Oh, I don't know."

"Come on, Garth. After what's happened with the soldiers at his place and ours, you don't seriously expect Stan's going to turn up here at sunset with his weekend bag packed and a pair of horses, do you?"

"I suppose not."

"So. We're agreed. We're going to use the oxen and we're going to set off now."

"All right, Arnie. If you think that's best. I'll go and get them ready. Anything you want me to put in the cart?"

There were some muffled sounds as though something was being handed over but in the dim light Edwin couldn't see what it was. The sky was only just beginning to show faint pink tinges of dawn. He saw the vague outline of the one he presumed was Garth walk past the window towards the oxen's stalls.

Just at that moment a rooster let rip with a loud "Cock-a-doodle-dooo!" Edwin nearly jumped out of his skin.

Next minute there was a commotion from the hen coop. Edward heard another "Cock-a- . . . " which stopped as abruptly as it had started, followed by noisy clattering and the flapping of wings and a great deal of squawking.

Granny appeared beside him in the pile of hay.

"Fox got in the hen house," she announced.

"Cock-a-doodle-dooo! Cock-a-doodle-dooo!"

"Well, one survived, at any rate. What did you find out, Edwin?"

Edwin quickly related the conversation to Granny.

"Did you find out where they're going?"

"No. They never said. They just said 'the camp'."

"So the only way to find out is to follow them. And they're going now, are they?"

"Yes."

"And you say Garth's gone to prepare the cart. Well, that's good news for us. We'll keep an eye out for the other one – Arnie, did you say it was?"

"That's right. I think Garth must be his brother. Arnie talks to him like he's an idiot. Really bosses him about."

"Well, as soon as Arnie is aboard the cart, we'll make so bold as to borrow their house to have our breakfast in."

It wasn't long before they saw Arnie follow Garth into the barn. Granny and Edwin stayed hidden in the pile of hay. There was a lot of scuffling and stamping of hooves and the sound of Garth's voice giving commands to the oxen as he led them out of the other side of the barn and yoked them up to the cart.

Granny didn't feel it was safe to emerge until they heard the creak of cart wheels setting off. Then they scrambled out from their hiding place, picking bits of hay out of their hair.

"I'm going for another reccy. You go indoors. If there's a fire burning, try to stir it up a bit. Just try not to set the place alight."

And with that Granny was gone, back round the far end of the animal shed.

Edwin ventured forward and into the house through a gap in the sacking. The room was dark but he could see the embers of a fire on a small hearth in a corner. The whole place smelled smoky. There was some wood stacked nearby so he carefully put a couple of small pieces on the fire and poked at them with a longer branch until they started to blaze.

Granny nodded approval as she came in.

"Well done, lad. We'll make a Boy Scout of you yet."

"What did you find out?"

"I nipped back on the roof, where we hid last night. That side of the roof looks out over the yard where they keep the cart. It's right on the edge of the lane. You can see from up there how the road winds round in a great big loop and then comes back again.

"Oxen are good for stamina, but they're not fast. This pair don't even make walking pace. I can see why Stan would prefer horses for his get-away. But that's by the bye. What it means is, we can have a nice leisurely breakfast here and then a quick hike across the field and we'll catch up with the ox cart as it comes out of the loop."

"What are we having for breakfast, Gran?"

"These." Granny rummaged in the pockets of her bloomers and produced two large, brown, new-laid eggs.

"See if you can find a bucket of water and a small metal bowl."

Edwin managed to locate both without too much trouble. Granny put the eggs in the metal bowl, covered them with water and set the bowl on the fire. As soon as the water boiled she struck a very theatrical pose and started singing.

"What are you doing, Gran?"

"Timing the eggs. Don't interrupt me or they'll be overcooked. Find some spoons."

Edwin burst out laughing. Gran ignored him and carried on warbling away.

At the end of her song she used the hem of her apron to pull the bowl of boiling water and eggs away from the fire.

"I'm dreaming of a white Christmas."

"What, Gran?"

"The song. It lasts exactly three-and-a-half-minutes. Just how I like my eggs. Now, did you find any spoons?"

They had to manage without spoons but there was a hunk of coarse, dark bread on a shelf which Granny cut up into strips with her Swiss Army knife.

"There you go – boiled egg and soldiers."

Edwin had never tasted better.

"Do you want a drink now?"

"Please, Gran. What is there?"

"Well, there's the hot water but I'm sorry I can't oblige with a tea bag. If you'd prefer a drink of milk, hand me those two cups."

Edwin passed over two rough pottery beakers that stood on the table. Gran quickly rinsed them out with the hot water. Then she disappeared in the direction of the animal shed. Five minutes later she was back with two cups of milk.

"Where did you get those?"

"Milked the cow, of course. Didn't I tell you I was in the Land Army in the war?"

"Is it all right to drink it just like this?"

"Please yourself."

Gran downed a good gulp of milk and smacked her lips.

"That's better. I was parched. Try yours, Edwin. It won't poison you, I promise."

Edwin looked at his cup. They always had red top at home and kept it in the fridge. This milk was foaming and creamy and it was still warm from the cow. Gran was watching him so he took a careful sip. He couldn't believe it. This was a different drink altogether from the milk he was used to.

"Good?"

"Yes. Smashing. Thanks, Gran."

"Well, now we've had breakfast we'd better get ready to set off. Let's have a look at you."

Edwin stood up and Gran surveyed him through narrowed eyes.

"Not bad, not bad. Your shorts and fleece are okay but take your tee shirt off."

"What for?"

"Just do it. Now, turn it inside out and put in on again."

Edwin did so, looking confused.

"We don't want to draw attention to ourselves, do we? These people don't go in for fancy tee shirts. So you'd better not have a great big pattern on the front of you. Now, let's see what we can do to complete the disguise."

A search of the room brought to light a pile of drab, grey-brown, loosely woven material that looked like sacking and several bundles of coarse, uneven string.

With the help of the Swiss Army knife, Gran soon transformed a couple of strips of sacking into a shapeless tunic that hid Edwin's own clothes.

"Cor, it scratches a bit, Gran!"

"Never mind. It does the job." She set about making a shawl for herself.

Among the sacking material she found some that had already been made into bags.

"This is a find. We've got a good use for these. Put your foot out."

Moments later their trainers had disappeared from view.

"Our feet may seem a bit big, but otherwise they'll look just the same as everyone else's now."

Gran found one more use for a strip of sacking when she fixed it on to one of the bags to make a strap.

"Good shoulder bag, that. Ought to hold plenty." She handed it to Edwin. "Hold on while I make another one for myself. Never know when they may come in handy. Right, now, are we ready to go?"

Edwin nodded and Gran led the way out of the cottage and across to the field opposite.

In the distance they could see a small cloud of dust where the ox cart was moving slowly along the looping road.

"Off we go for a nice brisk walk, then. I should say it's about a mile. We ought to catch up with them in a quarter-of-an-hour."

# CHAPTER 6

The hedge surrounding the field opposite the cottage was a straggly affair, thicker in some places than in others.

"Look for a gap where we can push through, Edwin."

"Okay."

Edwin found a likely place and they shouldered their way into the field. Granny turned back and Edwin saw her reaching into a pocket in her bloomers for the Swiss Army knife. He wondered if there was a gadget for repairing holes in hedges so no-one could tell you'd come that way.

When Granny caught him up a moment later she had two Y-shaped sticks with her, each about as long as a school ruler.

"You carry on walking. I'll catch you up in a minute." Granny sat down and started undoing the strings on her sacking shoe covers.

"Go on, go on, I won't be a minute."

Edwin did as he was told. It was easy walking over the field. Sheep were cropping the short, springy grass. They looked a bit scraggy, not as plump as modern sheep but they were just as docile. They didn't even look up as he passed by.

Granny caught up with him very soon.

"I've made you a little present."

She held out one of the Y-shaped sticks. She had tied a piece of elastic so that it hung in a loop between the two top pieces of the Y.

Edwin took his stick.

"What is it, Gran?"

"It's a catapult." Gran had made one for herself as well. She held out the elastic and pulled it taught, then let it twang against the stick.

"Don't tell me you've never played with a catapult?"

"No, Gran. I don't think mum'd let me have something like that."

"I consider a catapult a necessary part of your education, a boy of your age. Here, let me see how good your aim is." Gran bent down and picked up a couple of small stones.

Granny put one of the stones in the middle of the elastic, gripped it tight, pulled the elastic back and pointed the missile at the backside of the nearest sheep. When she let go the stone flew out and hit the sheep right on the tail. It looked round in surprise and Edwin burst out laughing.

"Go on, have a go." Gran tossed him the other small stone.

At first Edwin couldn't even manage to pull the elastic back without dropping his stone, but little by little he got the hang of it.

"Hey, this is great! How did you make them?"

"I cut the sticks from the hedge as we came through. Saw two nice, springy branches growing there and thought they'd do."

"Where did the elastic come from?"

"As soon as I got my trainers I took the laces out and replaced them with elastic. Saves me bending down to tie and untie them every time. Just slip my foot in. I kept the original laces, though. Never like to throw anything like that away. Got them here in one of the pockets in my bloomers. So I did a quick swap and used the elastic to make the catapults."

By the time they were to the other side of the field Edwin could not only hit a sheep, but he could aim for its foot or its tail and be pretty certain of being smack on target.

"It's the ideal place to practice, Edwin. You can't break any windows here."

As they approached the road they could hear the cart crunching towards them on its big, solid wheels. Edwin spotted a gap in hedge and they squeezed through.

As the cart came towards them Granny hobbled out into its path and Garth did the best he could be execute an emergency stop.

"Whoa, my Flower! Whoa, my Sunshine! Whoa, up!" The cart swayed and creaked to a halt and the oxen stood still, flicking their ears.

Garth stared down at Granny and Edwin.

"What is it, lady? What do you want?"

Granny lifted a hand to shade her eyes from the early morning sun and fixed her stare firmly on Garth. She spoke directly to him, ignoring Arnie, at his side.

"I see you are going our way, kind sir. Would you be so good as to give us a ride with you? You see, I suffer from such a swelling of my feet, I find it hard to walk far. My grandson has the same affliction. We should be very grateful, kind sir."

Arnie scowled and shook his head, making it clear he didn't want passengers.

Without a word, Granny turned away, let out a great sigh, bowed her head and began to limp painfully along the road ahead. Edwin tottered after her, trying to look as though his feet were killing him.

Garth immediately called out to them:

"No, no, it's all right. You can ride with us, lady, you and the boy."

"What are you doing?" Edwin heard Arnie hiss at his brother, "We don't want them with us."

"We can't let an old lady with bad feet walk. It's not right, Arnie."

"Oh, thank you, thank you, kind sir. God bless you. God bless you, kind sir." Granny bowed and scraped and nudged Edwin ahead of her as she shuffled to the back of the cart.

Arnie was still grumbling under his breath at Garth.

The cart was low and flat. Granny and Edwin had no trouble hoisting themselves up.

"Gee-up my Flower! Gee-up my Sunshine!"

Garth called to the oxen in a sing-song voice and cracked his whip. The two huge beasts strained to get the cart moving once more. As soon as it was rolling they got into their stride and plodded steadily forward. At every step a small puff of dust billowed up from under their feet.

Edwin and Granny propped themselves up on some sacks and sat with their feet dangling over the edge of the tailboard, as the cart trundled slowly along. It was a beautiful morning and the birds were singing.

"You comfortable, Edwin?"

"Yep."

"Good. Now just remember, keep your voice down. We don't want them to hear us talking. We mustn't draw attention to ourselves. As well as having bad feet, it's better if they think we've both got sore throats as well."

Edwin grinned. He probably would end up with a sore throat if he whispered all the time.

"So where are we going, Gran?"

"We're going down a hill."

"Yes, I can see that."

"And we're travelling west at the moment."

"How do you know?"

"Because the sun rises in the east. We're sitting on the back of the cart facing the way we've come, and we've got the sun in our eyes, so we must be facing east. Therefore, the oxen are facing west."

"Right."

"And I think it might be worth looking out for a junction of some sort."

"Why?"

"Well . . ."

Gran glanced over her shoulder to make sure Arnie and Garth weren't paying them any attention.

". . . in our day, a couple of miles west of my house and towards the bottom of a hill there's a busy round-about."

Gran's reckoning was spot on because they very soon came to a T-junction. Edwin looked out for a signpost but there was nothing to show where the roads led.

The cart veered off to the left.

"Do you know where we're going now, Gran?"

"We're going in the direction of the place I know as Tilkington, but we shall have to wait and see if that's where we end up."

"What's it like?"

"It's a little market town. The main street is terribly steep. You'd be wise not to ride down it on a bicycle unless you'd checked the brakes. There's a church at the top, and a big Co-op. Only I don't expect that's there today."

"I wonder if that's where the camp is?"

"We'll know soon enough."

"How far is it?"

"About three miles."

"Wouldn't it be quicker to walk?"

"Yes, it probably would. For us. But don't forget we've got good sensible shoes on under this sacking. You can see the state of the road, all ruts and rocks. Suppose you were only wearing your socks. Would you fancy walking three miles on a road like this?"

"No, I suppose not."

"Well, most people round here will only be wearing sacking socks. You've got to be pretty wealthy to afford shoes."

"Don't their feet get cold in the winter?"

"Yes, I'm sure they do. I don't suppose you know what chilblains are, do you?"

"No, Gran."

"When I was a girl, everybody had chilblains in winter. Sores on your toes caused by the cold. I bet these people get chilblains on their chilblains when it's really bitter."

"Gran, you know when we were listening in the loft? Did you hear them talking about Winchester?"

"Yes, I did."

"I live in Winchester. What were they saying about it? I know there's a big statue of King Alfred in the town – him who burned the cakes. Were they talking about him?"

"No. Not King Alfred. He was Anglo-Saxon. They were talking about another king who came after him, who didn't like the Saxons at all."

"Who was that?"

"Do you remember, when the soldier came to the door he shouted 'Open up in the name of King William'?"

"Oh, that's right, he did."

"He was talking about King William the first. Better known as William the Conqueror. Winchester was still the capital of the kingdom in his day."

"So how long ago are we talking about, Gran?"

"The better part of a thousand years."

"Wow!"

"Do you know anything about the Battle of Hastings?"

"Not really. I might have heard of it, but that's about all."

"William came here from Normandy in northern France in 1066 and there was a big battle at Hastings on the south coast between the Normans and the Saxons. The Saxon king, King Harold, he got killed and William and the Normans won the day. William was crowned king of England on Christmas Day 1066."

"So is that where we are now – back in 1066?"

"No, I think we're about twenty years on from then. William set up this big survey of all his possessions in this country in 1086. That's what's known as the Doomsday Book."

"Was that the survey Stan and the others were talking about, before the soldiers came?"

"That's right. It covered every household, all the farms, animals, mills, fishponds, beehives. Stan and his cronies were right, it was done to raise taxation. William was red hot on that.

"That's what Stan and his pals are so angry about. They are going to have pay tax to a Norman landlord on everything on the list. Under King Harold, some of the Saxons owned their land and homes in their own right but when William came, he put his Norman knights in charge and gave them lands that previously belonged to the Saxons. That's the cause of the resentment. They now have to pay tax to a Norman over-lord on property that once belonged to their own family."

"So are Arnie and Garth and the others Saxons?"

"I believe so. And it's best if they believe we're Saxons, too. That'll be no problem, because as luck would have it, Edwin is a good old Saxon name. Did you know that?"

"No, I didn't."

"We shall have to be careful if we fall in with the Normans."

"Granny, what did they say that you got so excited about?"

"They mentioned someone named Kinmer. He is their lord of the manor. Now, the place where I live is called Kinmers Lea, Edwin. They were talking about the man who gave his name to my village. That convinced me we are still in the same place but in a different time."

"They mentioned another lord – someone Stan said was the king's son. Who's he?"

"Lord William Peverell. He was, or I suppose I should say is, the Governor of Nottingham Castle."

"What, is he the Sheriff of Nottingham, like in Robin Hood?"

"He might be if he lives long enough."

"What do you mean?"

"If you remember, Robin Hood is given permission to marry Maid Marion by King Richard. In the film that was Sean Connery. A fine figure of a man."

Granny stopped speaking and Edwin noticed a strange, dreamy expression on her face. She suddenly snapped back to herself again.

"Where was I? Oh, right. That was King Richard the first. Only he won't be born for another hundred years.

"There's a story I always liked about King Richard the first. He went off to fight in the crusades and was captured and held to ransom. No-one knew where he was so his friend, the minstrel Blondel, went round all the castles singing Richard's favourite song outside the walls. Eventually Richard heard him and joined in the chorus, and that was how he was discovered. I always thought that was a nice little tale."

"But that hasn't happened yet?"

"No. Yes. Well, it all depends. If we're talking about today, on the back of this cart, with Arnie and Garth, no. It hasn't."

"I do find this time thing confusing, Gran."

## CHAPTER 7

The cart continued along its way, rocking about on the uneven road surface, the wheels following the ruts that had been cut by all the previous carts going that way. There was no other traffic on the road and nothing on either side but fields. Some were cultivated, some had sheep or cattle grazing in them.

Edwin had his catapult in his hand and was practising taking pot shots at targets along the way. Periodically he jumped off the cart to pick up a handful of pebbles to use as ammunition. He could hit a tree every time. Hitting an individual branch or leaf was more difficult when he was on board the cart because it jolted about such a lot.

Once he hit a bird flying past but he had to admit that was by accident. He'd actually been aiming at a fork in a tree branch only the wheel went down a pot hole at the crucial moment. To be honest, the bird got in the way of his stone.

He felt bad about hitting it. He couldn't tell if he'd killed it because it fell on the far side of the hedge. He tried to convince himself it was probably only stunned and would be able to fly away again.

While Edwin was feeling guilty about hitting the bird, Granny started rummaging deep into the shoulder bag she had made herself.

To Edwin's amazement she produced a chicken.

"Is it dead?"

"Of course it is. Don't you think you would have heard it making a bit of a fuss if it wasn't?"

"What are you going to do with it?"

"You enjoyed your chicken casserole the other night. I thought we might get the opportunity for another."

"Where did it come from?"

"Out of the hen coop at the back of the cottage."

"So it wasn't a fox?"

"No. It was me."

"And did you . . . you know . . ."

"Kill it? Yes, I wrung its neck. Remember . . ."

"I know. You were in the Land Army. But I didn't know that meant you were good at killing things."

"You can't eat meat without killing things, Edwin."

Granny spread the dead chicken out on her lap and started pulling out the feathers and throwing them off the back of the cart.

"What are you doing?" Edwin was aghast.

"I'm plucking it."

"Ugh!"

"How do you think the feathers get off a chicken? Do you think they fall off, like autumn leaves dropping off a tree? Sorry to disappoint you, Edwin. Someone has to pull them out. And this is how it's done."

Gran's gnarled old fingers flew over the corpse. Edwin watched in fascinated horror as the chicken's skin was revealed and the trail of feathers continued to fall behind the cart.

Gran reached into her bloomers pocket.

"I think you'd better look away now, Edwin."

He quickly did so. He heard the sound of the Swiss Army knife cutting through flesh and bone. There was more rummaging in pockets.

Edwin kept his gaze fixed firmly over Garth's shoulder, studying the oxen's wooden yoke.

"It's all right. It's safe to look again."

The chicken was transformed. The head and legs had disappeared and the plump pink body was all trussed up ready for the oven, just like you'd buy in the supermarket.

Gran gave a satisfied little nod and put the chicken back in her shoulder bag.

"That'll be nice, later."

The thought of eating the chicken made Edwin feel sick. Over the next ten minutes he gave careful thought to converting to be a vegetarian. There was the problem that he hated vegetables but that didn't matter. He had no appetite for anything at the moment.

Arnie and Garth rode along in silence. Gran kept an ear cocked, hoping to overhear any conversation between them but the noise of the wheels on the road drowned out any chance of that.

Occasionally they could hear Garth calling out to the oxen, encouraging them along. He used a particular sing-song tone of voice that carried over the crunching of the cart wheels. If he spoke to his brother at all, it was too quietly for Gran and Edwin to hear.

The first sign of interest on the journey was when the cart rumbled past half-a-dozen rough looking huts.

"Is this a village, Gran?"

"I suppose you could call it that. Though it hardly warrants the name. More like a hamlet, at best."

"Do you think anyone lives here?"

"If they do, they're keeping well out of sight."

Nothing and nobody was stirring.

Granny stood up and faced the front of the cart.

"Nobody up and about yet in these parts, driver!" she called out.

"Happen the soldiers came this way last night and this morning folks don't trust the sound of hooves on the road."

"Ahh! There's no-one in Alderswood with an ounce of guts in them!" Arnie spat over the side of the cart.

Granny sat down again. She had got what she wanted.

"Alderswood, Granny. Do you know where that is?"

"Indeed, I do. We're on the road to Tilkington, all right. The next village should be Cottesale, where Stan comes from."

"How far?"

"About another mile."

As they got close to the next village Edwin put his catapult away in his shoulder bag and stood up on the back of the cart to look ahead. What he saw brought him back down beside Gran in double quick time.

"Up ahead, Gran, there's been a fire. A hut's been burned down. You can still see smoke."

Gran got up and they stood side by side, looking down at the devastation. As they drew level with the smouldering remains of the hut, Garth slowed the oxen to a halt.

"Whose home was that, then?" Gran enquired.

"Athel . . . " Garth began, but his brother cut him off sharply.

"Nobody we've heard of. We don't know the folks who live in these parts."

Arnie was making it plain there would be no further discussion of the burned out hut. Granny and Edwin returned to their seats on the back of the cart.

There was a muttered exchange between Arnie and Garth as the cart re-started its slow, deliberate progress and Garth began to gee the oxen up to greater effort.

"Did the soldiers burn his house down, Gran?" Edwin kept his voice to a whisper.

"I expect so. When they didn't find him at home. Stan probably saw the flames as he made his way back to Cottesale and realised what had happened. I'll bet he's going to make some-one pay for this. We've got to try and find him."

"But we don't know where he's gone."

"He's gone wherever this cart's going. We've got to stick with Garth and Arnie like glue."

The cart moved on fractionally faster for a minute or two and then reverted to its original speed. However twitchy Arnie was feeling, they were not going to get to their destination any quicker than the oxen would plod.

"I'm wondering what they'll do when they get to Tilkington, Edwin. That hill's far too steep for two oxen to drag this cart up. And I wouldn't fancy going down the hill. These things don't have brakes, you know."

"What do they use to stop them with, then?"

"The oxen will stop on the flat when they get a command from the driver. They stop walking and the weight of the oxen holds back the weight of the cart. When they go downhill, their horns take the weight of the wooden yoke and the cart behind it. But two oxen wouldn't be able to hold back the weight of this cart on a steep hill like Tilkington main street. It would run away with them."

"So where do you think we're going?"

"I don't know but I don't reckon we'll be going up or down that hill."

They were not even on the outskirts of Tilkington when the cart stopped again.

"This is it. We can't take you any further." Arnie's voice barked out.

Edwin jumped down on to the road and was preparing to walk on when Granny grabbed his sleeve and pulled him back. Next moment she had thrust the oven ready trussed chicken into his hand.

"Creep up on Garth's side of the cart and put this on the driver's seat beside him. Try not to let Arnie see you."

Edwin squirmed with disgust at the touch of the dead chicken, but he swallowed hard and slunk forward, holding the chicken behind his back.

"Oh, kind sir," Granny began in her most wheedling voice. "How can we ever thank you for your generous help. We would have struggled to get this far without your kindness. God bless you, good sir. God bless you."

Edwin tiptoed to the front of the cart. He reached up and pushed the chicken on to the seat beside Garth. He gave it an extra little shove to make sure Garth noticed it was there. Then he scuttled back and climbed aboard again beside Granny.

"We only have another mile to walk. Together, me and the boy will support each other as best we can. Two cripples together, hobbling along the weary road. God bless you, sir. Good bless you."

Garth flicked the whip.

"All right, mother. You can come with us into Tilkington. Stay on until we get off the cart."

He began calling to the oxen again to move forward. Arnie hissed at him angrily but his words were drowned as Granny began another loud round of thanks and blessings.

Edwin was grinning to himself and punching the air as the wheels started to turn and they moved forward.

"Well done, Gran!" You persuaded him to let us stay on board."

"Right. And I bribed him with his own chicken, if he did but know it."

# CHAPTER 8

As they strained forward, one of the oxen – Flower, as it happened – dropped a huge, smelly cowpat. Edwin and Granny got the full benefit of the stink when the cart passed over it.

"Pooooh!" Edwin held his nose.

"There's nowhere to hide, Edwin. Why don't you jump off the cart for a minute or two. Have a walk. Or go and see what you can find in that field. They look to me like juicy young carrots growing there. Here . . ."

Granny rummaged among the litter in the middle of the cart and fished out a pointed stick she had noticed among the other oddments.

Edwin took the stick and was only too glad to get down and away from the smell.

There was no hedge so he had no trouble getting into the carrot field. He managed to dig up half-a-dozen carrots with his stick. In the next field he noticed a row of some other green vegetable tops sticking out of the earth. Curious, he dug one of those up too and carried it back to cart.

"What's this?"

"Well done, Edwin. That's a leek. Very good for flavouring, those are. Go nicely with chicken."

Granny carefully stowed all the vegetables in her shoulder bag.

Edwin wondered where they were going to get another chicken from. Whatever happened, Granny would have to catch it herself. There was no way he was going after it.

"I'm thirsty, Gran."

"I'm afraid there doesn't seem to be a buffet car on this service."

Edwin grinned.

"Sorry, Gran."

"I tell you what, there's an apple orchard over there. Go and help yourself to a few, but don't let anyone see you."

Edwin nearly filled his shoulder bag and was chewing a sweet, juicy apple when he caught up with the cart again.

He polished one on his sleeve and handed it to Gran.

"Thank you, Edwin. I hope you enjoyed your first scrumping expedition. You seem to have got the hang of it."

Edwin laughed and moved to hop up onto the back of the cart. Too bad Sunshine had just followed Flower's example, and as he stepped forward he put his foot into the biggest cowpat he had ever seen.

"Oh, yuk! How am I ever going to get it off this sacking stuff?"

He scrambled aboard and tried to scrape his foot on the edge of the cart but all that did was rub the cowpat everywhere. It seemed nothing could stop it soaking into the sole of his sacking sock.

Edwin travelled on in miserable silence. Granny was concentrating on chewing her apple. Edwin guessed she didn't have any helpful suggestions to offer him.

"You were just in time with your scrumping. Look's like we're not alone any more."

For the first time since they started out, they had met another cart on the road. It wasn't long before they were at the end of a line of carts heading into town.

They arrived in Tilkington at a T-junction about half way up the steep hill. All the carts were pulling off the road into a kind of lay-by where a couple of scruffy young lads dressed in sacking were moving among the animals, giving them water and putting on nose-bags full of feed.

Garth swung their cart round and parked it neatly in a corner. Arnie was obviously anxious to be off the cart and away as fast as they could but Garth fussed around the oxen, scratching their noses and talking to them. Both brothers ignored Granny and Edwin completely.

Edwin watched Garth go over to one of the young lads. He pointed towards their cart and gave some instructions and then handed over a coin. Arnie was already at the corner of the parking lot, fretting to get going.

Just when it seemed he was ready to leave, Edwin watched Garth turn back to the cart and carefully stow the oven ready chicken under the driver's seat and cover it up with a bit of sacking. Then he joined his brother and they made their way towards the steeply sloping main road.

"Edwin, run after them and see which way they go!"

As he set off, Edwin saw Granny poking around among the sacks and bundles on the cart. He wondered what would end up in her shoulder bag this time.

It was only a short distance to the main road. To Edwin's surprise, there were tables set out up and down the street, like market stalls, and people wandering about between them. He could clearly see Arnie and Garth heading up the hill. That was all he needed to know.

He headed back to Gran with his report and set to work dealing with his most pressing problem.

"What are you doing?"

"I've got to get this stuff off my foot, Gran. It stinks. I can't walk about with it. It's vile."

"Well, make sure no-one sees what you've got underneath your sack socks."

Edwin spotted a puddle and waded into it, kicking his feet about in the dirty water. He didn't care about getting his sack socks clean, just so long as he got the smell off.

He stamped his feet to dry them and then shuffled after Gran who had started walking slowly towards the main street. She was limping and somehow it didn't seem to Edwin that she was putting it on. It looked like she truly did have pains in her joints. Not surprising, really. The cart ride had been pretty bumpy.

"All the fun of the fair, Edwin." Gran was enjoying herself, as they wandered among the food stalls. The fruit and vegetables were small and not very evenly shaped but they looked fresh.

There were baskets of eggs, neat piles of hazelnuts and walnuts, chunks of sticky honeycomb. There were oven ready chickens, trussed up like the one Granny had given to Garth. There were even live fish and eels in great crockery pots.

Edwin looked at the other stalls. All the stuff looked as if it had been left over from a very poor quality car boot sale. Thick, clumsy pottery bowls. Hefty leather straps and buckles. Wood carved into quaint shapes. Cumbersome tools with massive blades and handles. He noticed a wooden rake that looked as if it would take two men to lift it.

"Still thirsty?" Gran nodded towards a stall selling milk out of a wooden barrel.

"Yes. But we haven't got any money, have we?"

"Come with me a minute. I want you to stand by this stall and not move until I come back."

"Okay."

They went up to a stall selling pottery. There were dishes and bowls and mugs without handles. Gran put on her most persuasive voice as she approached the stall holder.

"I'm sure you'll have no objection, good sir, if I borrow some of your pots."

Before the stall holder could react, Gran had three mugs in her hands and was thanking him profusely.

"I shall leave my grandson here as a surety until I return them to you. In fact, I'll not take them out of your sight. You have a little space right here, on the end of your table, and that will be just perfect for my purpose.

"Now," at this point Gran raised her voice and addressed everybody passing by, "who can tell me which cup contains the lady?"

With a flourish, she produced a walnut, which she must have taken off the nut stall as they passed by.

Everyone in the vicinity stopped what they were doing to gather round and watch.

Gran put the walnut down on the table and up-ended one of the mugs over it. Then she quickly slid that mug aside and put another in its place.

Keeping all three mugs in a row, she slid them from first position in the line, to second, to third, muddling them up so fast that it was impossible to keep track of which mug was which.

"Where is she now?" she cried. "Who would like to wager me which mug she'll be under? You, sir? You want to find the lady? Well done, the first to try!"

A small coin was passed forward through the crowd, which was quickly assembling around Gran and the upturned mugs. The hopeful contender named his mug, Gran lifted it for all to see that there was nothing at all underneath. Then she quickly moved the mugs around again and revealed the nut, under a mug where nobody had expected to see it.

"Would any one else like to try? Who will wager me . . .?"

This time, several hands in the crowd were raised and several more coins were passed forward. But nobody could spot the 'lady' under the correct mug.

Edwin watched in amazement as Gran fooled them again and again. And still there were more who wanted to try their luck. And were willing to pay for it.

At last, Gran called a halt. She thanked everyone for playing the game and the crowd drifted away. Gran stashed most of the coins away in one of the pockets in her bloomers. She turned back to the stall holder.

"How much for the three mugs. I rather think I'd like to keep them?"

"You keep them, lady, and take my blessings with you. That was a wonderful show you put on for us. Kept everybody guessing and enjoying themselves. And several bought from me, while they were standing here. If you'd like to come back and do the same show again later on, I'd be very pleased to let you use space on my table again. And do keep the mugs."

Gran thanked him graciously. Edwin felt her hand on his shoulder as she steered him away and through the throng, back to the milk stall. They used two of the mugs for their drink of milk.

"Now we've had our elevenses, I think we'd best try and catch up with Arnie and Garth. You said they went up the hill?"

"That's right. How much money did you make, Gran?"

"I've no idea."

"What?"

"Well, do you know what these coins are called or what they're worth. Because I'm blowed if I do."

"Have we got enough money to buy another chicken? They've got some for sale over there."

"What would we do with two chickens?"

"Pardon?"

Granny patted her shoulder bag.

"We've already got a chicken, Edwin. You didn't think I'd leave Garth's chicken behind on the cart, did you?"

At that moment they heard a commotion coming down the hill. A squad of armed men was moving through the market searching all the stalls, pushing people aside, poking into boxes and baskets, peering under counter tops.

They could hear angry voices raised in protest:

"What are you looking for? Why are you turning the place upside down? What's the matter?"

"A young woman is missing, with a young child. If any of you is concealing her, it will go badly with you."

"Who? Who is it? Who's missing?"

"Edith de Kinmer and her son, Robert."

# CHAPTER 9

"Gran . . . Gran, they've done it. They've taken them already. We're too late!"

"Then we must try to find out where they've gone. Come on, we haven't got a moment to lose."

Granny and Edwin set off up the hill as fast as their legs would carry them. It was a steep climb and the back of Edwin's legs were aching. He put his arm out for Granny to lean on.

Towards the top, the road curved round to the right. The camp was set on a broad, flat area at the top.

Everywhere, men were working. Some were tending fires, or animals. Edwin noticed horses and goats as well as oxen. Other men were busy with balks of timber or great sheets of leather. There was activity and noise everywhere, not to mention more strange and horrible smells.

They stood at the edge of the camp and surveyed the scene. It was a jumble of permanent and temporary buildings, wooden shacks and hovels and an assortment of tumbledown creations of sacking on poles and more solidly constructed tents made out of thicker material.

"This looks to me like an army on the move, Edwin. If not a whole army, then at least the commanding officer and his retinue. And I think I can guess who the commander will be."

"Some Norman lord?"

"Lord Peverell himself, I expect. And if he is here, it's very likely Lord Kinmer is, too. I think I can see the logic of the kidnap plot now. Kinmer and his family would be much more vulnerable here in this make-shift encampment than in their own home in the village."

"If Lord Peverell's here, will they let people just wander about?"

"Can you see any sentries, or people showing passes to get in?"

"No, Gran. But there are soldiers poking about over there, like they were down in the market."

"But they don't seem to be restricting entry to the camp. Let's try our luck, see what happens. We don't want to draw attention to ourselves. Stick close and try to look casual."

Edwin gave Gran his arm again and she leaned on him quite realistically as they approached the nearest of the structures. No-one challenged them as they shuffled forward.

"Keep your eyes peeled for our two chaps. Stan mentioned someone called Bebba working as nurse-maid to the baby. I expect she will be in one of the grander tents, seeing as the baby's father is lord of the manor."

They moved around the site, avoiding the searching soldiers, and peering in every direction, but they couldn't spot Arnie and Garth.

It was difficult to make progress in any one direction because there were no streets or lanes. Everything was higgledy-piggledy and they constantly had to back-track to walk round someone chopping up wood or milking a goat.

"Gran! Do you think that's them over there?" Edwin had spotted two sandy haired men ahead.

Gran stepped away from him and craned her neck for a better view.

At that very instant, Edwin felt a huge, hairy hand grab him round the arm and drag him away from Gran's side. The force was so great it almost lifted him off his feet. He stumbled over his sacking socks and had to grab his shoulder bag to save losing all his apples.

He called out but the huge hand dragged him behind a thick leather flap, away from the main press of people.

"Gran . . . help . . ."

He was deposited in a heap on the ground beside a great roaring fire. Red hot embers spilled out everywhere and he was afraid his sacking clothes would catch alight.

A huge figure towered over him, topped by a bushy, ginger beard. The man was naked to the waist and wearing a big leather apron.

"You boy. Take handle. Pump bellows. Don't stop."

"What . . . ?"

A kick in the backside was all the answer Edwin got. He fell forward onto his knees and he could feel the heat of the fire on his face. He scrambled up and tried to find a way out, back into the main part of the camp.

The heat was intense. The big ginger man in the leather apron was all he could see. He had lost all sense of direction.

Gran was outside, somewhere, on her own. Was she all right? Did she know what had happened to him?

The next thing he knew was a mighty cuff round the ear from a great calloused hand.

"Told you, lad! Pump! Now!"

The blow propelled Edwin forward and he collided with the handle of the bellows.

It was either grab it to keep himself upright, or fall in the fire.

He held on to the rough wooden handle, which came up level with his chest, and pressed it down. There was a whoosh of escaping air and the flames danced up higher.

"Good! Pump more! Heat furnace. Smith needs fire."

Edwin seemed to have no choice but to carry on pumping the bellows.

As the furnace blazed up, the smith reached forward towards the fire with a great pair of tongs. He used them to take hold of a piece of metal sticking out of the fire and pulled it, red hot, from the flames.

Holding it in the tongs, he rested it on an anvil and began beating at it with an enormous hammer. Sparks flew off the metal in all directions. Edwin was sure his tunic was burning because he could smell it, but he could do nothing about it.

Next, to his amazement, the smith lifted the piece of metal off the anvil and plunged it into a barrel of water that stood next to the fire. Steam flew out with a mighty hiss, and water sprayed everywhere.

Edwin was terrified. He tried to dodge as hot water splashed onto him. The thought went through his panic-stricken brain that at least his clothes couldn't catch fire if they were soaking wet.

Edwin looked round frantically. How was he going to escape from this hell-hole? The smith was between him and any possible way out, taking up all the space in the small enclosure around the fire.

The smith's chest and arms were streaming with sweat and he was brandishing a hammer bigger than any Edwin had ever seen.

The smith seemed to be glorying in the heat and the steam and the stench of molten metal. He threw back his great shaggy, ginger head and laughed aloud as he took up another strip of metal and plunged it into the flames.

"Ha! Ha! Good, eh?"

"No. No. I want out of here. What about my Gran. She's outside on her own. She needs me. I have to get back to her . . ."

He might as well have been talking to the wall. The smith took no notice of him whatsoever. He was completely immersed in the thrill of beating at red hot metal and making the flames in the furnace dance higher and higher.

At the slightest sign of Edwin failing to push down on the bellows hard enough, he lashed out with hand or foot and unless he wanted to be bruised all over, Edwin had to keep pumping.

This was unendurable. He was soaked through with sweat, his arms were numb from the effort of pumping, he was afraid every minute he would stumble and fall in the fire.

From an easy-going ride on the back of a cart with his Gran, in moments his life had been transformed into terrifying misery.

What would happen if Gran couldn't find him? Would this monster of a smith keep him working the bellows forever? How long could he last at the job, in the heat and the grime and the constant fear of falling into the shimmering embers. One false step and he would be among them, and they would consume him in an instant.

Just as he felt he was reaching the limits of his endurance, without warning a figure burst through the leather screen and pushed past the smith. Edwin felt himself grasped by the wrist and dragged away from the fire and behind his captor to safety.

"Leave him be!"

To Edwin's amazement, it was Garth's voice, shouting in the smith's face.

"You've been told before, Wulfric, you must take a prentice. Pay a lad to work for you. You can't just grab a boy off the street and put him to labour for you. Let him go!"

Next moment Edwin was back out in open air and Granny was fussing over him, wiping his face.

"Oh, Edwin, are you all right? I wondered whatever had happened to you. Garth here, when I ran and told him you'd disappeared, he seemed to guess what had happened and came right back over with me. He said he'd get you out. We're very grateful to you, kind sir."

But Garth was already on his way back to his brother, some distance away. He seemed to think the chicken payment enough for the rescue as well as the ride.

"Let's have a look at you, now. You're clothes are all singed, and your hair, and you've got such a dirty face. Are you all right? Are you hurt?"

"No, no. I'm fine, Gran. Really. Now I'm out of there, I'm okay."

"So you've stopped worrying about the smell of cowpat on your socks?"

Edwin laughed out loud and Gran gathered him up in her arms in a hug.

In truth, although he couldn't admit it to Gran, Edwin didn't know whether to laugh or cry, he had been so scared. He could hardly have lasted any longer with that terrible smith with the mad eyes, who laughed at the flames and the red hot metal. Horrors had gone through his mind when he thought Gran may not be able to find him.

Whatever happened, from now on he had to make sure he and Gran didn't get separated again.

# CHAPTER 10

Gran was anxious not to let Garth and Arnie out of their sight so they made their way after them as quickly as they could.

The brothers were moving further and further into the encampment. Granny and Edwin dodged from the cover of one tent to another, gradually catching up with them.

"Look, Gran. I'm sure that's Arnie's sleeve sticking out from behind there."

They watched for a few moments. The sleeve hadn't moved in that time so neither, presumably, had Arnie. There must be a reason for him to be standing still. He must be talking to someone, but they were too far away to overhear any conversation.

Gran looked round.

"We need to find somewhere we can hide where we can listen in on them without them knowing we're there."

She spotted a likely hideout.

"Come on."

Edwin was not impressed. It involved crouching down behind a couple of horses that were tethered close to where the brothers were standing.

"Do we have to hide right here?"

Edwin could do without horses just like he could do without oxen. The only small thing in their favour was that horses didn't have horns.

Gran brushed aside Edwin's objections and they manoeuvred themselves into a position where they had a perfect view of the two brothers, who had been joined by a woman.

"That must be Bebba!"

"I expect so. I wish she'd turn round so we could see her face."

They didn't have long to wait before the woman made a dramatic movement and twirled round. She was dark haired and might have been quite pretty if it hadn't been for the angry scowl on her face. As her shawl fell aside it was evident that she was very pregnant.

"So. The woman they chose for nurse-maid will be nursing a baby of her own soon."

"If she's having a baby herself, Gran, how could she think of taking someone else's child away from them?"

"That depends on how much she hates her, doesn't it?"

Edwin couldn't guess what a burning hatred it must be.

"It looks as if there's been a change of plan, and the kidnap happened without their help. Otherwise they wouldn't be standing about chatting. We need to hear what they're saying. Let's try to move closer, where we can overhear them."

Edwin was all in favour of that.

He was much happier hiding inside a heap of hay, until he realised he was squidged up between Gran and a rather hungry donkey that kept pulling out big mouthfuls of the hay from all round him. He tried not to listen to the grinding noise the donkey's teeth made as it chewed.

He edged further forward. He didn't want to be too close when the donkey went for its next mouthful.

"No. We've not seen or heard from Radfred or Wiglaf either, since they all left our house last night. We came on impulse, Bebba. We felt sure Stan must have made his move and would expect us to come after him. But I assure you, he left us no message."

"Impulse!" Bebba spat. "Just like a man. Make all these elaborate plans and then at the last minute throw them to the winds and act on impulse. You're useless, the lot of you!"

"What else was he to do? We saw the cottage burned to the ground as we came by Cottesale on the cart. He must have seen smoke in the distance and realised what was afoot."

"My home's destroyed and my man's gone off on some fool's errand with no strategy and no assistance. And I suppose I'm the one that will have to sort it all out!"

"Did you see nothing of him, Bebba? Did he not leave you a sign?"

"The sign he left me was an empty crib! Baby gone, mother gone, no trace of either of them. Who else would it be but my Stan who took them? That was exactly what he was planning to do – only tonight, after dark, was what we agreed, not before noon-day!"

Gran was practically leaning out of the hay pile in her eagerness to hear more.

"What did I say, Edwin? Stan has already snatched the victims. I wonder where has he taken them."

Garth and Arnie stood shaking their heads but saying nothing, while Bebba continued her story.

"I'd only left her and gone outside because she sent me out to look for mushrooms. Said she had a fancy for mushrooms for her lunch, if you please. The little madam! So out I go, and when I come back they're gone."

"You're sure she hadn't just taken the baby out for a walk?"

"Are you mad? Do you think her lord and master would allow her to walk around the camp with his precious son and heir. Why do you think they hired me? I'm the one that takes him out for walks and feeds him and changes him and quietens him when he cries. She sits about acting high and mighty, handing out her orders, cool as you like. As if she was anyone I ought to obey! The insolence of her!"

"Did you raise the alarm?"

"No. To begin with, I confess I did wonder if she'd taken a little stroll, just nearby, you know. I poked my head out to see but there was no sign of her.

"Then I went to look in her lord and master's office. When he's supposed to be there, often as not he'll be skiving off to spend time with her and the child, instead of attending to other matters. Paperwork and the like. I wondered if she'd gone to pay him a visit. But neither of them was there. Then I really did wonder if they'd made a little excursion together. So no, I did not raise the alarm. Then he comes in and asks me where she is.

"'Why, my lord,' says I, 'I thought she was with you.' Then he gets agitated and says no, he's not seen her since breakfast time. He asked where I had been and I told him about going out for the mushrooms — on her instructions, I told him. I had the mushrooms there, so there was no question about it.

"It was Kinmer himself that raised the alarm. He sent for Ralf Giffard and told him to take over his duties because he was going outside to look for his wife. He asked Giffard for one or two of his guards and sent them off looking round the camp, too. I was instructed to wait here in case she made her own way home. When they all came back empty-handed, she was declared kidnapped and the baby with her and the hue and cry was on."

"We saw the soldiers searching the market, didn't we Gran?"

"Shhhh!"

"The only report was of a man seen nearby with a horse. But that meant nothing. There's enough horses about here. It could have been anybody."

"The thing is, Bebba, what has he done with them?"

"I don't know! I know what we planned, but it's my guess that has fallen apart, like everything else. Your guess is as good as mine, where they are now."

"Wait a minute, Bebba." Arnie was trying to calm the situation. "We believe it's only because the soldiers were on to him that he came and put the plan into action early. If they hadn't made their move, Stan wouldn't have changed anything, I feel sure. You're too hard on him."

"Pfff!" Bebba tossed her head.

"He only altered what he had to. The timing. It's my guess he will have stuck to the rest of the arrangements, just as agreed."

"You think?"

"I do. It was a good plan. Bringing it forward is the only change he's made up to now, isn't it? Nothing else. What reason would he have to deviate from the rest of our intentions?

"He's a man. I don't expect him to need a reason to deviate from anything."

"Without any knowledge to the contrary, I think we must assume he's taken them to the caves under the castle, like we said."

Granny and Edwin both reacted so violently they nearly fell out of the pile of hay in their excitement. The donkey backed off as his meal seemed to be having convulsions.

"If that's the case, then I must go to him." Bebba was wrapping her shawl round her and looking as though she expected to set off that instant.

"Wait up, wait up . . ."

"No, Arnie. I'll not wait. If that's where my husband is, then that's where I shall be. You were the one so definite about sticking to the plan. Well, that was the plan — that we should be there together."

"How are you going to get there?"

"You've got transport. You said you came on the cart."

"Do you want me to go and get the oxen ready?" At last Garth seemed to find something he could talk about.

"No. Not yet." Arnie's tone was definite. "Let's lie low and set out tonight, after our evening meal. That way, we'll be back to our original schedule. Besides, it'll look suspicious if you leave right now, Bebba. You should go back inside and act up a bit, you know, worried about your mistress and the little one. Ask what you can do to help."

"All right. Come back for me later, when the camp's settled down after sunset. Meanwhile, you'll see what a great display I can put on."

Bebba spat on the ground and laughed a malicious laugh.

## CHAPTER 11

"So we're going to Nottingham Castle by the looks of it, Edwin."

"Good-o!"

"But we won't go until dark. So in the meanwhile, let's look round a bit more. This seems to be the part where the important people are to be found."

They were deep in the central area of the camp. Here, it was less hectic than on the perimeter although there were still plenty of people moving about. But the raucous din of the smiths and carpenters and leather workers was quieter here. It was easier to hear people speaking although sometimes their words were not clear.

"I can't understand what these people are saying, Gran."

"That will be on account of some of them are talking French."

"Why?"

"Because they come from France."

"But they're not in France now. They're in England. Why don't they speak English?"

"Because the Normans won the war so they can speak any language they like. And if the locals know what's good for them, they'll learn a bit of French, too."

"Can you speak French, Gran?"

"A little. Ern petty purr."

"What?"

"That's French. That was me speaking French. Don't you do French at school?"

"No. Did you learn it at school?"

"No. I was with the French Resistance during the war. Took a crash course before I was parachuted in behind enemy lines."

"Really?"

"Yes. I told you. I got about a bit during the war."

"Teach me some French."

"It might be a good idea for you to know a few words. Let's start with 'please'. See vuplay. Say it."

"See vuplay."

"Very good. And 'Thank you' is mehr-see."

"Murr-see".

"No. 'Mehr' with a good rolled arrrrh! Like you're trying to get rid of a frog in your throat. Mehr-see."

"Mehr-see."

"Excellent."

"Another good one to learn is 'Let's get going'. That's Ali vuzon."

"Ali vuzon."

"Very good."

Edwin grinned.

"See vuplay. Mehr-see. Ali vuzon. I can speak French!"

"You need to learn 'yes' and 'no'. 'No' is Nor."

"Nor."

"That's right. And 'yes' is wee-wee."

"Are you sure, Granny? You're not having me on?

"Edwin, it's true. I swear it."

"Maybe."

They had wandered past the back of several tents but now found themselves facing the open flap of a large marquee that looked as if it was for some kind of official use. At the further end a man was sitting at a long table littered with parchments and overflowing boxes of what looked like the odds and ends out of the bottom of a school desk.

The marquee was as untidy as the desk, the floor cluttered with sheepskins and horses' harness, odd bits of soldiers' uniforms, wooden poles, buckets and flagons.

Granny drew Edwin to her side behind a pile of empty boxes where they could peep in but not be noticed by the man.

He was a burly, red faced, middle-aged man with hands the size of plates with big, fat fingers. He was clearly a soldier because he was dressed in a uniform of chain mail. His metal helmet with the spiked top and nose guard was on the desk beside him.

He looked to be in a bad mood. He kept mopping his brow with his hand and periodically he let out an exasperated sigh or hiss of annoyance.

One after another, he pulled the parchments in front of him, studied them for a moment and then tossed them aside again. Occasionally he reached into one of the boxes and fished something out and made a mark with it on another piece of parchment which he kept by him. He was clearly not happy about what he was reading because he kept shaking his head and crossing things out that he had just written down.

Eventually he got up and stamped out through a flap at the corner of the tent and they could see him making his way to another tent nearby. He disappeared inside and came out a few moments later with a big metal cup in his hand. The way he tossed the drink down and gave a little growl of satisfaction as it hit the spot, it could only be beer.

When the cup was empty he disappeared and was soon back with another. A second man followed him out and they started up a conversation. They were too far away for Granny and Edwin to catch what they were saying.

"Stay here a minute," Granny instructed, and to Edwin's surprise she darted forward into the deserted marquee and grabbed something up off the floor. In next to no time she was back beside him with a bulge under her skirt that was far too big to be something in one of the pockets of her bloomers. Granny didn't offer any explanation and Edwin got the distinct impression he wasn't expected to ask.

They waited a while but the red faced man didn't come back to his desk.

"Who do you think he is, Gran? Could he be Lord Kinmer?"

"He has this marquee to himself and he's clearly doing some office work, so I suppose he could be Lord Kinmer, although I imagine he'd rather be out searching for his wife."

"He doesn't look very friendly, does he?"

"No. But still, his wife and child have been kidnapped so you've got to feel sorry for him."

"We're going to try and get them back for him, aren't we?"

"Indeed we are, Edwin. We'll do everything we can to get Edith and her little boy to safety. But before we set off on our mission of rescue, there's something else we have to do."

At that moment there was a movement very close to where they were hiding.

"Quick!" Granny hitched up the bulge under her skirt and darted away among the maze of tents, Edwin right on her heels. They took a zig-zag course until they came out at the other side of the beer tent.

"That was a near thing. We almost got caught then, where we probably shouldn't have been. Let's move back towards the edge of the camp where people are less likely to notice us."

Gran picked an area where some of the market people had set up cooking pots over campfires and were preparing their evening meals.

Edwin had a wistful thought of chicken casserole. Ah, well. With no way of cooking it, Garth's chicken would stay in Granny's shoulder bag.

In a gap between two family groups Granny and Edwin sat down and made themselves comfortable on the ground. Gran got into conversation with their neighbours and in no time one family had passed across half a bucket of water and the other group had provided some embers so that Gran and Edwin could start a fire of their own.

Gran thanked them very much and, following their example, scooped out a hollow in the ground for a fireplace. She sent Edwin to find some wood to keep the little blaze going.

"Don't wander out of my sight, mind!"

"No chance of that, Gran!"

He kept looking back every few seconds as he searched. He noticed other people collecting off-cuts from a pile that had been left by one of the timber workers earlier in the day. Making sure he never lost sight of Gran, he hurried over to fetch an armful.

When he got back he couldn't believe his eyes. In the middle of their little fire was a metal pot containing the trussed chicken surrounded by slices of carrot and leek, all boiling away merrily.

"Hurry up with that wood, lad. We don't want to let the fire out. I'm afraid I can't oblige with dumplings tonight. I do apologise."

"Gran."

"Yes?"

"You're wonderful!"

Edwin bent and kissed her on the cheek and she smiled up at him.

"Who lent you the pot, Gran?"

"Nobody. I pinched it?"

"You what?"

"I pinched it out of that marquee."

"I knew you came out with something but I didn't notice a stew pot in there."

"Neither did I. But I'm afraid one of the soldiers will be in terrible trouble when he has to go on parade. He'll learn not to be so careless about where he leaves his helmet in future."

# CHAPTER 12

After families had eaten, the circles round the campfires opened up and several family groups joined together. Edwin and Gran were invited to sit along with the people nearby. Gran accepted on their behalf.

They settled down among the folk from the market. Edwin tucked his feet under him and pulled his sacking close over his clothes but nobody was taking very much notice of him.

Some of the men got out playing cards and several enthusiastic games were soon in full swing. The women were taking the opportunity to catch up on the gossip of the day. Some of them had small children in their laps and were rocking them to sleep as they chatted.

A young man produced a penny whistle and began to play. At first it seemed a mournful melody but as the player got into his stride his tunes speeded up. Soon some of the younger people were on their feet, dancing. Edwin sat among them all, fascinated and delighted by the easy-going, enjoyable company.

Gran got up.

"You'll be all right here for a minute or two, if I just have little wander, won't you?"

"Don't go far, Gran. Don't leave me on my own for long."

"I promise. I'll be back in a tick."

Edwin noticed Gran stoop to speak to a woman sitting nearby who looked over towards him and nodded vigorously. He guessed Gran was asking her to keep an eye on him. He felt better when he knew that and went back to watching the dancers in the flickering firelight.

Gran was as good as her word. She came back shortly after, carrying a couple of fresh oat cakes wrapped in a twist of hay and half a flagon of goat's milk.

"We need to be off now, Edwin, otherwise we may miss our lift to Nottingham. I've found us something for breakfast. Here, you carry the flagon.

It's got a bung stuck in the top but it's not all that secure. Mind you don't spill it."

She tucked the oat cakes into her shoulder bag and checked their little area of ground to be sure they had left nothing behind.

Edwin got up and took charge of the goat's milk. He was sorry to be leaving the camp fire and the penny whistle man and the laughing dancers. Gran seemed to feel the same. They stood a moment longer, enjoying the happy scene.

"Come along. We must go." Gran raised her voice. "Goodnight to you all."

"Goodnight! Goodnight!" followed them down the hill towards the deserted market.

"Hang on, Gran. I can't see a thing!"

When they turned away from the firelight it took several minutes and a few bruises to his shins before Edwin's eyes adapted to the darkness. In fact, there was an almost full moon. As he got used to picking his way in the strange, silvery light, Edwin became more adept at avoiding obstacles in his path.

Gran was going along at a cracking pace, never tripping over anything. She seemed to have total recall of their route, although Edwin had only the vaguest idea of where they were going. He knew it was down the hill, but that was about all.

Gran veered off the main road and it took Edwin a moment to remember how they had walked through from the parking lot.

As they neared the place where they had left the cart, they could hear a subdued mumbling and rumbling from the oxen, most of whom seemed to be awake and chewing.

"Do they eat all the time, Gran?"

"They're cows. They chew the cud."

"What's that?"

"You know a cow has four stomachs?"

"You're kidding me?"

"No. It's true. Four stomachs. Don't laugh, Edwin. It's not a joke."

"Nothing's got four stomachs, except in science fiction!"

"I said four stomachs, not four eyes. The cow has to chew its food again every time it goes between one stomach and the next. That's what they call it — chewing the cud."

"How do they do that?"

"Believe me, Edwin, you don't want to know. Look, Flower and Sunshine are still here."

"Oh, yes."

Gran walked up to their pair of oxen and scratched their noses.

"What are we going to do, Gran? Are we going to stow away on the cart?"

"That's certainly an option, but I think we'd be in trouble if they discovered us before they set off. We'd end up having to walk to Nottingham and I don't fancy doing that. No, I've got a better idea. When we hear them coming, you take my arm and we'll set off walking slowly ahead of them."

It seemed a long wait before anyone else came near the parking lot. Huddled up in shadows by the wall, keeping out of sight in the moonlight, Edwin wished they could have stayed by the campfire for longer.

At last they heard footsteps. It turned out to be a false alarm. One man on his own, a person they had never seen before, came and fetched his cart and led his oxen out on to the road before climbing on to the driver's seat and cracking his whip. The sound of the wheels scrunching over the stones had long died away before there was any other sign of life.

Finally, they heard a group of people approaching and this time there was no doubt it was Arnie and Garth with Bebba.

"Quick, before they spot us."

Gran and Edwin slipped away in the shadows and hurried along the road. In the still night, the sounds of Garth's preparations to get the cart moving carried clearly to them. They could hear him calling to the oxen in his special, sing-song voice, geeing them up and getting them to take the strain of a standing start. At last, they were under way.

"Come on, now's our chance. In the middle of the road and hobble as much as you like!"

Edwin held out his arm and Granny clung to him, acting the part of a lame old woman to the hilt. She could barely put one foot in front of the other without nearly pulling him over. Edwin thought the groaning and wincing was a bit overdone.

"Whoa there my Sunshine! Whoa my Flower!" Garth brought the cart to a halt right behind them. "Is that you, good mother? Where be you going at this time of the night, you and the boy?"

Granny turned, acting surprised to see him, as if she was trying for an Oscar.

"Why, bless me if it isn't that good, kind gentleman with the cart we encountered before. We have to get to Nottingham by morning, good sir. 'Tis a long way, so we need to start early to get to our destination."

"But it'll take you all night. It's much too far for you to walk. I can't let you do that, not with your bad feet, an' all. Besides, it's dangerous on the road in the dark, you and the boy alone. Here, get up on the tail of the cart again and we'll carry you. I don't know why you didn't come and ask again for a ride."

"Oh, no, good sir. I wouldn't presume. You've been too kind to us already. It's more than anyone has a right to expect. God bless you, sir. God bless you."

Arnie and Bebba were spitting with helpless rage up at the front of the cart as Garth got down from the driver's seat and personally escorted Granny and Edwin to the back. He lifted them up and made sure they were properly settled before he went back to the oxen and the hiss of angry voices up front.

"What do you think you're doing? We don't want them with us!"

"Who are these people? Do you know them?"

"'Tis only a poor old dame and her grandson. We let them ride with us before and they were no trouble. The old lady has the most terrible deformity of her feet and the boy has inherited the same thing. And I think he's a bit simple in the head too."

Edwin sat up, open-mouthed to hear that.

"Wulfric the smith grabbed him today and nearly had him in the fire. The boy didn't even know to keep out of Wulfric's way as he walked by his smithy. All the lads know Wulfric and his ways. 'Twould only be one soft in the head who would be taken so."

Granny looked at Edwin and raised her eyebrows. She leaned close and whispered:

"Being an idiot could be a very useful thing to plead in future, if you get into trouble. You've already got a witness that you're half-witted."

Edwin laughed.

"I'll remember that."

"It's going to be a long ride, Edwin, right through the night. We may as well get some shut-eye."

"Okay, Gran."

They pulled their feet in over the tailboard of the cart. Granny fussed about with the sacking until she had made a comfortable cushion for herself and a bed for Edwin. She settled herself down.

"Good night, Edwin. Sweet dreams."

"Night-night, Gran."

Edwin curled up beside her and in moments the juddering and jolting of the cart had rocked him to sleep as sweetly as if he had been a baby in a pram.

At one point in the night he half woke but quickly subsided back again into sleep. Pink sugar mice were nibbling at his hair while a brass band, comprised of soldiers in chain mail, played 'Rudolph the Red-nosed Reindeer' as a grizzly bear chased him round a bonfire.

Later, he almost surfaced again but sleep claimed him back immediately. He was hanging on the end of a rope, down a well, listening to a baby crying, while a troupe of oxen in green wellies danced the can-can on the roof of his mother's car.

Just as dawn was breaking Granny shook him gently.

"Wake up, Edwin. Wake up."

He opened his eyes and peered up at her blearily.

"Sit up, then. Here's your milk and oatcake. Did you have a good sleep?"

"Yes, thanks, Gran." Edwin raised himself on one elbow. "Did you?"

"I dozed a little, here and there. Did you have any nice dreams?"

"No, Gran. I don't remember dreaming at all."

# CHAPTER 13

When they arrived in Nottingham, Edwin could see immediately that it was a big, important place. The houses were solidly built, not flimsy lean-to's and tents, like the camp. The people were better dressed and went about their business in a more purposeful way.

There was no atmosphere of jollity like there had been in the market. This was the main town of the county and the most important men in the locality lived and worked here. They were Normans and they would see to it that the Saxons knew their place and kept to it. There was a definite atmosphere of control about the place.

There was one main thoroughfare with many smaller streets and lanes leading off it. The main road was jammed with carts full of produce, men on horseback and riding donkeys, herds of animals being driven along – sheep, cattle and goats.

"Market day," Garth commented, in a resigned way. He leaned back in his seat and picked his teeth as he looked round at the bustle going on in every direction.

"We'll stay with them until they get off," Granny whispered.

They had the best part of an hour to admire the scene unfolding around them as more and more people came thronging through the gates into the city. Eventually, Garth was able to find parking for the cart and the same ritual was enacted as the previous day, with a coin changing hands and a youth running forward with a bucket of water and two feeding bags.

Bebba was impatient of the delay and never stopped grumbling to Arnie and Garth, complaining about everything and everybody.

"I've got a nice little treat tucked under my seat," Edwin heard Garth telling her, in an attempt to sweeten her temper. "We shall have a good dinner when we get back tonight."

"I don't eat a bite until my man's restored to me!" Bebba tossed her head and her dark, untidy curls swirled round her shoulders.

Bebba seemed to have forgotten Granny and Edwin were there. They slipped away before she remembered and started asking questions.

In the city they found it easier to keep close tabs on Bebba, Arnie and Garth without being noticed. They dogged their footsteps all the way to the big outcrop of sandstone known as Castle Rock, that dominated the city. There were trees round the bottom of the rock but the summit jutted up high above the surrounding treetops.

The road sloped ever upward towards the castle that was perched on the very top.

Bebba, Arnie and Garth reached a point where they had to either go forward into the castle precincts or leave the road. Granny thought it advisable to back-track and watch from nearby until they were certain what Bebba and the two men intended to do.

"Didn't she say the caves under the castle, Gran?"

"That's right."

"So they won't go inside the castle, will they?"

"I shouldn't imagine so, but I don't know how they'll get down to the bottom of the rock without going in. I can't see a path. Can you?"

With the tall trees and, lower down, a tangle of undergrowth, Edwin couldn't see a path either.

The group of three had come to a halt ahead of them. They were too far away to be heard but it looked as if the two men seemed to be trying to dissuade Bebba from something. Even at that distance it was plain that she had an obstinate face and was going to do exactly as she chose, whatever they said.

Finally, Arnie and Garth walked away from her. They came and sat down on a large lump of stone uncomfortably close to where Gran and Edwin were hiding among some bushes. Gran tugged Edwin's sleeve and they drew back a little to avoid being seen but listened as hard as they could.

"The woman's mad as a ferret in a sack. She'll listen to no reason. She'll get us all hanged."

"She's concerned for her husband, Arnie. Is natural."

"She's concerned that he's brought her the hostages so she can start looking forward to the money she'll make when she names her price for their release."

"Do you think he will pay up for them?"

"The lord of the manor's wife and child? You bet he will! And plenty."

"Isn't it enough of a punishment to him, to think they are taken away? Does Bebba need to look for a ransom as well? Isn't it sufficient to scare him a bit, teach him a lesson that we're not as soft as he thinks we are, and then give them back?"

"She'd say you're too tender-hearted, Garth. What's wrong with a bit of cash for out-of-pocket expenses?"

"I don't know. I never liked that part of the plan. Seems it goes too far. We have a point to make about losing our heritage to a Norman upstart. We can do that without demanding money too."

"Bebba would never see that. She wants a new shawl. And a new bib for the baby. It won't be long coming, now. There's always expense there. You know they have three already so Stan won't say no to money in his hand."

Garth fell silent.

Suddenly Edwin spotted movement among the trees on the cliff side below the castle ramparts.

"Gran, look – over there. It looks as if someone's climbing down. It must be Bebba but it's difficult to see."

"Wait a minute." Gran rummaged in a pocket in her bloomers and pulled out the Swiss Army knife. She opened out gadget after gadget until she came to the one she wanted.

"Here. Look down this little tube."

"What is it?"

"It's a mini-telescope. See what you can spot through it."

Edwin took the Swiss Army knife and tried to find a way to hold the telescope to his eye without poking his other eye out on something sharp and spiky. He was seriously worried about the corkscrew.

Finally he found a safe way to hold it and peered down the little tube, turning a ring half-way along its length until the tiny figure of Bebba jumped sharply into focus, making her way quite confidently down the cliff face in regular steps.

"I think there must be some kind of staircase cut in the rock, Gran. She knows where she's going all right, and it seems easy enough for her to get down."

"Let's have a look."

Edwin handed the telescope over and Gran squinted down the tube.

"Oh, yes. I've got her. I think I can see where she's heading. Big
cave about two thirds of the way down. So that must be where Stan's brought them."

They passed the telescope back and forth between them, following Bebba's progress down the rock face. Edwin had the telescope when she arrived at the cave's mouth.

"She's gone inside. I wonder how long she'll be. Then we'll have to wait until she climbs back up and comes to report to Garth and Arnie."

"Unless they go to meet her, in which case we must make sure we're within eavesdropping distance."

"Quick, Gran, look! She's coming out."

Gran grabbed the telescope and stared through it.

"Oh, this doesn't look good. She's got a face like thunder. She's coming back up as fast as she can. She's waving now. Giving the thumbs down."

Gran frowned as she lowered the telescope from her eye.

"Do you know, Edwin, it looks as though she hasn't found them. They're not there."

Edwin stole a glance at Garth and Arnie. No wonder they were not responding to Bebba's signals. They'd both nodded off.

Edwin and Gran took turns again to watch Bebba climb back up to the level of the road. Edwin saw her turn in their direction and start to hurry towards them, trying to attract the men's attention by waving as she came.

Suddenly he gasped. Two soldiers had stepped out from either side of the path and grabbed hold of Bebba. He could see her struggling but they were much too strong for her and she was quickly overpowered.

"Gran . . . Gran . . ."

Edwin pressed the telescope into Gran's hands, speechless with shock. Bebba's arrest was totally unexpected. She must have been under surveillance all the time she was climbing on the rock.

So did that mean Arnie and Garth . . .?

He had no more time to speculate, as four more soldiers stepped out of the shrubbery and surrounded the two brothers. Arnie and Garth had a rude awakening from their doze. They had a spear in their face and their hands manacled behind their backs before they knew what was happening to them.

"Time to go, Edwin." Gran closed the Swiss Army knife and popped it back into her bloomers pocket. She got to her feet. Edwin did the same.

At that moment, four more soldiers emerged from nowhere and loomed up beside them.

# CHAPTER 14

Edwin trudged along in a daze. He couldn't believe what was happening to him. Granny had been bundled off with Bebba by a couple of other soldiers and he was being herded along with Arnie and Garth towards the castle. Neither of those two was saying anything.

The soldiers were the only ones enjoying themselves.

"Well, well, well. What have we got here? Your pals Radfred and Wiglaf told us you'd be stopping by, likely, some time today. And your mate Athelstan and his missus. Quite a little party."

Oh my god! Fred and Wiglaf had been arrested too and brought to Nottingham for questioning. And they had admitted that Garth and Arnie were planning to come to Nottingham Castle with Stan and Bebba. Those were the plans that had been set up at the meeting in the cottage that he and Gran had eavesdropped on.

How could they have given the names? Edwin couldn't believe it. These men had sworn to be true to each other.

The soldiers seemed to delight in taunting their captives:

"It took a bit of persuasion to get your names out of those two but they obliged at the finish. They always do. We've got ways and means in our dungeons here. Come along now. We'll see what you've got to say for yourselves when you get in front of the Governor of the Castle."

Wiglaf and Fred must have been tortured, right here in the castle. Edwin didn't dare dwell on what might have been done to them.

One of the soldiers gave him a poke with the handle of his spear.

"The gate man said you and the old woman were on the cart with the others, so you're under arrest, too. Come along. Don't make any fuss or it will be the worse for you."

Arnie and Garth walked in silence. It occurred to Edwin that they must have thought they were safe after the cottage was searched and nothing found. They had no idea of the danger ahead when they came into the city. They thought they would be able to go about whatever business they chose without being challenged.

To discover they were wrong, and were at this minute passing through the portals of a huge, fortified castle with very little chance of coming out again alive, seemed to have left them in shock.

Edwin's shock was only matched by his terror. What were the soldiers going to do to him? Would they try to get information from him? Could he tell them anything they didn't know already?

They knew who all the conspirators were.

But they didn't know Stan was on the run. It seemed Fred and Wiglaf didn't know that either, because they had told these soldiers Stan would be coming here with Bebba.

But the soldiers who came and searched the cottage, while Gran and himself were in the loft, were looking for Stan so they knew he'd gone into hiding.

It seemed impossible to Edwin that the soldiers had stumbled on knowledge of the meeting at the cottage by accident. Surely, they must have had a tip off. Perhaps the men had talked about their plans in less private places and been overheard.

Edwin wracked his brains to remember the details of the conversation that went on in the room below while he and Gran were listening up above.

Wiglaf had harboured a grudge against someone he thought was responsible for him getting a big tax bill. Maybe that was who had pointed the finger.

Edwin could remember Wiglaf suggesting they should go after Lord Peverell but Stan had said no, it would be madness to plot against him.

They were going after Kinmer's family, because he was the local lord of the manor.

Perhaps one of their neighbours in Kinmers Lea, who knew how much they hated the Normans, had been pressured into accusing them. These soldiers who were marching him into the castle seemed very willing to use 'persuasion', as they called it, to get testimony.

The very worst of it was that they had marched Granny away with Bebba and he didn't know where they were going to take her. He had determined that nothing would separate them again, yet here he was, on his own, frightened for himself but frightened for Gran, too.

He took his courage in both hands and shuffled forward and plucked at the sleeve of the guard who was leading them.

An iron-clad face turned back to him, only the eyes and mouth visible and neither smiling.

"What are you going to do with my Gran?"

"The women prisoners are confined separately from the men." The soldier pushed Edwin roughly in front of him.

"You're coming with us. I'm keeping my eye on you, so don't try any tricks."

Edwin found himself leading the sorry little procession towards the cells. The soldier gave him a poke in the back every few steps to make sure he kept up the pace.

They walked through courtyard after courtyard, until at last they came to a tall, wooden wall. It looked as though it could be opened wide to let a cart through, but there was a second, small door in the bigger one. One of the soldiers stepped forward and unlocked the small door and pushed Edwin forward, with Arnie and Garth on his heels.

In the darkness behind the door, Edwin stumbled down a narrow, uneven staircase, round a corner and into what felt like the jaws of hell itself.

What hit Edwin before anything else was the stink. Edwin's nose had been gradually getting used to the ripe smells around the market and the camp but this was a stench unlike any other he had ever known. He retched and thought he was going to be sick.

There was already quite a crowd of men inside. The source of the terrible smell was an indentation in the middle of the floor which seemed to serve as a toilet, without, apparently, ever having been cleaned in years.

The only window in the foul underground cell was a small opening near the top of the wall, covered with an iron grille. It was stifling hot. Edwin could hardly breathe.

The men crammed inside were avoiding the cess pit as far as possible, which meant constant jostling to keep their feet out of the disgusting mess around it.

As the newcomers were thrust into the cell, the crowd parted so that they had nowhere to go except straight into the vile, slimy mess.

Edwin tried to hang back but the place was so crowded it was impossible. He knew he was going to pass out, squeezed in among all these big sweaty bodies and the noisome stench from the lavatory.

As his legs sagged, to his amazement a pair of brawny arms caught him and lifted him bodily off the floor. The crowd parted momentarily and he was aware of a sea of filthy faces and dirty, greasy hair. Then everything went black.

He came to, he had no idea how long afterwards, light-headed and completely disorientated. The terrible reek of the cess pit was still in his nostrils.

His arms and legs felt as though they were wrapped in material and when he tried to sit up, he couldn't. As he struggled to raise his head, everything swung about at crazy angles. He could see the rough boards of the roof of the prison cell only just above his head.

Was this some bizarre instrument of torture he'd been put in? Were they trying to get information out of him? What would they do next?

He gave up trying to understand what was happening to him. He stopped struggling and let himself go floppy. The dizzy, swinging sensation gradually stopped. He tried to stay as calm as he could and get his bearings.

He could hear the men below him muttering among themselves but he couldn't catch anything they said. He seemed to be in the same cell as he'd been put in to start with. Perhaps it wasn't a torture chamber. But what was he doing, trussed up like Granny's oven ready chicken, hanging up near the ceiling?

It gradually dawned on Edwin that someone had taken pity on him and rescued him. As the smallest and weakest person in the cell, he would certainly be the one to fall into the cess pit first. No doubt the soldiers would find that a great laugh.

But someone had lifted him out of the stinking mire and rigged up some kind of hammock for him, off the floor, so he didn't have to slip and slide about in the muck in the company of all the men.

Even if he was still locked up and the evil smell was still making him vomit, at least he was not struggling for a foothold at ground level.

His saviour could only be Garth. Edwin felt a rush of gratitude and at the same time a pang of guilt about the chicken supper. Not that Garth was likely to know what he was missing, if things went against him here.

What would they do with Garth and his brother? How long would they keep them here? Would they be put on trial?

He fought to keep his brain and his memory clear.

The soldiers had said Wiglaf and Fred had given up the names of Garth and Arnie as plotters. What had happened to Wiglaf and Fred? Were they here in the cell?

Wiglaf had talked about bringing down Lord Peverell. Was that the charge against them all? Edwin had a feeling that any man accused of going after Lord Peverell wasn't going to walk away from it.

But Garth and the rest were in a difficult position to deny it. Their only defence was that they were plotting against another lord instead. Either way, it didn't look good for them.

What was he going to be charged with, himself? Was it a crime to hitch a lift on the back of an ox cart?

If the owners of the cart were insurgents against his lordship, it probably was. Lord Peverell was the king's son. After the king, there wasn't anybody more important than him. Just saying 'Good morning' to anyone plotting against him would probably carry the death penalty.

There was nothing he could do until someone came and told them what was going to happen.

Edwin was thankful, for the moment, to be off the ground, but he had absolutely no doubt that he was in greater danger than he'd ever been in his life.

# CHAPTER 15

Later in the day the soldiers came back. Edwin was tipped out of his hammock and marched away with Garth and Arnie.

They were brought into one of the large courtyards where a crowd was gathered. A raised dais had been set up containing a long table with chairs, facing into the central arena.

Seated in the middle of the table was a very commanding man. He was dark and good looking, his hair well cut, beard trimmed, his clothes clean and well-fitting. He was the first well turned-out civilian Edwin had seen. This was obviously one of the Norman lords. And since this was Nottingham Castle, Edwin had a strong suspicion that it was Lord William Peverell himself.

He was not such an old man as Edwin had imagined the Governor of the castle would be. He didn't have any grey in his hair or beard. He looked fit and athletic.

Edwin had barely obeyed the soldier's order to stand still, when Granny and Bebba were escorted into the arena from the opposite side.

Bebba tossed her head back and dragged away insolently from her guard. Edwin couldn't catch what she said, but it looked as if she was serving up some pretty strong insults. The soldier had her by the upper arm and shook her as he brought her to a halt, trying to insist she stay where he had put her.

Granny, on the other hand, was bent nearly double. Edwin's heart leapt into his mouth as he saw her. What had they done to her? She looked so stooped and crooked, he couldn't believe it was the same Gran who had marched so purposefully up the hill to the camp, only yesterday.

Just at that moment she glanced over to him and his heart leapt as she gave him a huge wink. What a relief! This was Granny practising her acting again. Well, she would give them a good show, even if it didn't do much good.

Edwin couldn't believe this man sitting in judgement upon them hadn't see it all before. He looked too sophisticated and worldly-wise to be taken in by any charades of Granny's.

Various scribes and assistants fluttered round the central seat at the long table. Very soon they were ready and a tall, bald man with a voice like a drill sergeant stood up and announced that the trial would begin.

"Step forward, Bebba of Cottesale."

Bebba wrenched herself free of the soldier's hold and stepped up boldly to the line that had been put on the ground in front of his lordship.

"You are accused," the bald man continued, "in company with your fellow conspirators, of plotting the overthrow and death of Lord William Peverell, Governor of this castle and of the county of Nottinghamshire. How do you plead?"

"I've no knowledge of any such plot." Bebba shot back. "You can see my time is nearly due with this baby I'm carrying. I have nothing else on my mind but that. You should not listen to idle gossip of malicious tongues!"

The bald man ignored Bebba's remarks and ploughed on with his questions.

"Where is your husband, Athelstan?"

"If I knew that, I wouldn't be here in the city seeking him! I heard a rumour that he'd come this way and came to find him myself. I have no knowledge of his whereabouts."

"Where was he two nights ago? He was not home, was he? And neither were you. Why was that?"

"I'm in the employ of Lord Kinmer, working as nurse-maid to the new-born child. I was not at my home because I was with Lady Edith and the baby two nights ago. As to where my husband was, you will have to ask him that!"

Lord Peverell leaned forward.

"When we catch him, we will. Have no fear."

When he spoke, he sounded as polished and decisive as he looked. There was no mercy in his face or in his voice. He took over the questioning.

"Do you know these two men – Arnulf and Garth of Kinmers Lea?"

Bebba nodded.

"Aye. They're well know in these parts. They gave me a ride here on their ox cart. We got here this morning. That's how I came to be in their company."

"And the boy?"

"I've never seen him before last night. He and the old woman rode along on the cart." Bebba was dismissive, didn't even look at Edwin or Granny.

"I see." His lordship sat and looked long and hard at Bebba. His expression said that he didn't believe a word she said.

"I have it on good authority that you and your husband are well known for fomenting discontent with Norman rule in these parts and for advocating that Saxons take the law into their own hands when it suits them. I believe you were implicated in this plot right up to your pretty little neck. Which, in other circumstances, I would be very inclined to stretch at the end of a rope.

"However." Lord Peverell let the word hang in the air, making Bebba wait and wonder what sentence he might hand down instead.

"However, I cannot doubt your claim that you are soon to give birth. I am not a cruel man. I don't wish to be remembered for hanging pregnant women. That would look terribly bad. No, I have another punishment for you.

"You shall be taken from here and locked up and the key thrown away and the jailers told to forget you. The caves under the castle hold a special fascination for you, so I'm told. Well, then, that is where you shall be held. There will be no possibility of escape. You will remain there in solitary confinement until you starve to death. Next."

Bebba screamed and fought like a wild cat but the soldiers held her tight and dragged her roughly out of the arena. As she was taken away her voice echoed round the walls, cursing King William, Lord Peverell and all Normans.

His lordship took no noticed at all and the soldiers next paraded Granny in front of him. She stood there, tiny and bowed down. A whisper of interest ran through the crowd.

"Who are you?"

"Amelia Bloomer, your honour."

Edwin had to suppress a shout of laughter. Good old Gran!

"What is your part in this plot, dame Bloomer?"

"I have none, your lordship. I simply came this way with the carter because he was so kind as to offer a ride to me and my grandson, there. I suffer so bad with my feet, you see, as the boy does. And he's a little simple in the head, too. A great responsibility he is, for one as old as myself to care for. He's only ten years old, you see. Parents died when he was a baby and I've had charge of him ever since. No, no. We don't know anything about any plot, good sir."

Granny bobbed and curtseyed and grovelled in front of Lord Peverell until Edwin thought he would laugh out loud. He just had to hope she'd done a convincing enough job.

"And what is your connection to Bebba of Cottesale?"

"Why, none, my lord. I never saw her before yesterday."

"Ah. I see. I believe nothing of what that woman told me. And now you are telling the same lie, yourself. Obviously, there is complicity here. You've put together a tale between you and are determined to stick to it. I see we have another traitor in the ranks. You shall also be sentenced to death."

Edwin gasped.

"But I don't like to be seen hanging old women any more than pregnant ones. It goes against everything I've been taught of chivalry. So you shall suffer the same fate as your friend Bebba, except you will be incarcerated in the castle until you die of starvation. Take her away. Lock her up and lose the key. Next."

Edwin was stunned. He couldn't believe what he had just heard. He dragged away from the guard holding him, frantic to get to Gran. He wanted to shout and scream at Lord Peverell, make him change his mind. But the soldier who was holding him was too quick. A bunch of iron-clad fingers slammed across his face and held his mouth shut, and the grasp on his arm tightened.

Granny didn't even have a chance to look round at him before the soldiers moved forward and hustled her off through a door in the courtyard that led straight into the castle.

Edwin was distraught. He thrashed about in the guard's grip. He felt as though he was drowning. His anger and fear were close to hysteria and the guard's mailed fist over his mouth was nearly choking him.

He barely heard Lord Peverell examining Garth and Arnie about their part in the plot to kill him. The outcome was a foregone conclusion. Whatever protestations they made of their innocence, they were sentenced to death by hanging, at dusk that very day, in the market square.

"Your friends Wiglaf of Baddington and Radfred of Swinesgate passed this way only yesterday. They warmed the gallows for you."

Lord Peverell laughed as Arnie and Garth were led away, back to the cell block.

Edwin was left standing alone in the big arena, with Lord Peverell glaring down at him.

"Step forward, boy."

The soldier let him go, with a poke in the back. Edwin reeled forward.

Standing alone, without the soldier holding him up, he wasn't at all sure his legs would support him. He was shaking and his breath was coming in broken gasps, like a dog panting.

"They tell me," Lord Peverell began, with a smirk on his face and in his voice, "that you are a simpleton. Can you prove that to me?"

What? How could he prove he was stupid? Edwin decided the best course was to say nothing.

"What's your name, boy?"

When he tried to answer, it took several attempts before Edwin could make his voice work.

"Edwin . . . Bloomer, sir."

"Where do you come from?"

"Winchester." He'd said it without thinking. It probably wouldn't be at all the right thing to say here, in Nottingham.

"I see. You're a long way from home, in that case. And who is the king in Winchester, Edwin Bloomer?"

Oh, well. In for a penny, in for a pound.

"King Alfred, sir?"

Lord Peverell's smirk changed to a scowl. There was a ripple of disapproval from the onlookers.

"We mention no Saxon kings here, boy. Who is the Norman king in Winchester?"

"Er . . . King William, sir?"

"Uh-huh. Better. And who am I, boy?"

Edwin crossed his fingers before he spoke.

"Lord William Peverell, sir?"

"Good. Even a simpleton needs to know who rules him."

Lord Peverell looked round and picked out a face at random from further down the table.

"And who is that?"

Edwin felt on safer ground. It was the red-faced man from the marquee in the camp.

"Lord Kinmer, sir?"

There was a general guffaw of laughter from everyone at the table, Lord Peverell included.

"You think this is Lord Kinmer, boy?"

"Er . . . yes, sir."

"Tell him who you are, Ralf."

"I am Ralf Giffard, as everybody here knows!" the big red-faced man roared, laughing heartily.

Edwin was confused. Getting the identity wrong was no bad thing if it convinced the court he was an idiot, but if that man wasn't Lord Kinmer, which of them was?

"Is it the kalends today, boy, or the nones?" Lord Peverell shot at him.

Edwin couldn't guess what the question meant. In desperation he held up his hands and pretended to be counting on his fingers.

"Er . . . I don't know, sir."

"So you can't tell me today's date. I see."

There was more tittering and giggling at Edwin's ignorance.

"And how many oxen are there in a bovate?"

"A . . . what, sir?"

"We've heard talk in this court today of Alderswood and Cottesale and Swinesgate. In which wapentake are they?"

"Erm . . . No idea."

The audience was falling about laughing by now, obviously thinking Edwin was completely stupid. He wasn't having to act. He hadn't the faintest idea what the questions meant so he had no possibility of answering them.

"I'm going to offer you a sextar. What do you say to that, young man?"

"Er . . . er . . . " Edwin looked round helplessly, shaking his head. He didn't have a clue what Lord Peverell was talking about.

"So you don't care for honey!" His lordship laughed again. "What have you got in your bag, lad?"

"Apples, sir."

"Take out one and pass it to me."

Edwin fished an apple out of his shoulder bag and gave it to the nearest soldier who, in turn, passed it to Lord Peverell.

"This apple, Edwin Bloomer, will decide your fate," Lord Peverell announced. "I will have my finest archer strike it from the top of your head with a single arrow. He's usually an excellent shot. However, nothing is certain in this life . . . ha, ha, ha."

Edwin couldn't keep up with what was happening. What did his lordship mean? What was the archer going to do?

One of the soldiers was dragging him to the side of the arena, as his lordship pointed out the position where he wanted Edwin to stand.

"I'd provide a blindfold, but I don't know whether to offer it to you, or the archer!"

The crowd was going absolutely wild, clearly looking forward to some sport.

"Give me another apple." Edwin lobbed an apple to Lord Peverell who caught it deftly. He gave a signal and a tall, mail-clad archer stepped forward on the other side of the courtyard.

Lord Peverell handed the apple to one of the soldiers who took it and stood it on a barrel a little way in front of where Edwin was standing.

"Fire!" Edwin jumped as the arrow whooshed past him, splitting the apple clean in two.

"Have him stand by the wall and bind his hands behind him."

Edwin felt himself being man-handled across the arena. One of the soldiers tied his wrists and another squared his shoulders up against the wall and stood the apple on the top of his head. Then they both stepped clear.

"My archer has one shot. If he splits the apple, which, as you have seen, he is perfectly capable of doing, then you will walk free, young man. If, however, his aim should be a little less than perfect today, well, let us just say, that would be unfortunate . . ."

Lord Peverell signalled again and a drum roll began as the archer stepped forward to take his aim.

Edwin braced himself, determined that however much of a simpleton they thought him to be, he would die bravely.

# CHAPTER 16

The archer drew back his bow to its furthest extent and took aim. There was a hush in the crowd as the moment for his shot approached.

Then, in the silent heartbeat before the archer discharged his arrow, Edwin heard a sound that no-one else in that crowded arena could possibly recognise. The twanging of elastic.

It could only mean one thing. Granny's catapult in action. He didn't see the stone strike but everyone clearly saw the archer's hand fly up, out of control, as he released the bow-string. His arrow flew wide and buried itself harmlessly in the woodwork way above Edwin's head.

Pandemonium broke out. People all round the arena were waving their arms in the air and shouting. Lord Peverell was out of his seat, shaking his fist.

"Archer! Back to your mark! Fire again!"

The crowd began to boo, jeering and hooting.

"No! No!"

"He's had his chance. Let the boy go!"

"Fair's fair. One shot and he missed. Set the lad free!"

Then the chanting began. And between each chant, the stamping of a hundred feet on wooden planks underlined the message.

"Let. Him. Go." Stamp-stamp-stamp.

"Let. Him. Go." Stamp-stamp-stamp.

"Let. Him. Go." Stamp-stamp-stamp.

Lord Peverell sat down again. His face was like a thunder cloud but he knew better than to displease the crowd. He beckoned a soldier over to him.

Moments later, Edwin's hands were released and without ceremony he was taken to a small door in the side of the arena and thrown out into the street beyond. The door banged shut behind him.

Edwin's legs were shaking. They felt like jelly. He only got a few yards before he had to sit down on the ground. He could feel tears near and although he tried not to give way to them, he felt their hot splashes on his face. He couldn't get his breath. There was a burning sensation in his throat and he

158

knew he was going to throw up. His stomach was churning with great urgency.

On the opposite side of the street from where he sat, he could see a track that sloped steeply down and disappeared out of sight between clumps of bushes. It looked as though it would provide a bit of privacy which was what he most definitely needed. He got up and made his way unsteadily across the street and followed the track down.

He slipped and slithered through the undergrowth, lost his footing and landed on his hands and knees.

He lost all control of his stomach then, but he felt better when all the nasty stuff whirling round inside him was on the outside. He sat back and took several deep breaths.

He could hear running water. He looked around and to his left spotted a small waterfall that seemed to issue straight from the rock. He crawled out from under his sheltering bush and made for it. He reached across and stuck his head under the trickle and had a good long drink.

He washed his face and hands, and his hair. It was bliss to get rid of the smell and the yuk and as they rinsed away, with them went the worst reactions to his terrifying ordeal.

He had got out alive. That was the main thing.

Suddenly a tidal wave of exhaustion hit him. Then he leaned his back up against the rock wall beside the little cascade, let his head slump, and in moments was fast asleep.

When he woke, he had no idea how long he had slept, but he thought probably not long. The sun was not much lower in the sky and it still felt comfortably warm.

He had felt so utterly spent when he sat down, drained by the tension and fear of his trial in the arena. Now he was okay again. He jumped up feeling full of energy and ready to go.

The first thing was to find Gran. All he knew was that she was somewhere inside the castle. He had no idea which direction the catapult shot had come from but Gran must have had a clear view of the arena at that time.

But if they were going to lock her in a room to starve to death, would it be close to such a public place? More likely, she was on the way to her prison cell when she took the pot-shot. Edwin's most urgent task was to get back inside the castle and then start looking for Gran.

Getting back into the castle was probably not going to be easy. He'd just been chucked out, so the gate keeper was hardly likely to give him a free pass back in. But the main gate was the only way. After all, the castle was built with the idea of keeping out intruders. The walls were much too high to climb and the archers probably had orders to shoot anyone on sight who put a foot near the battlements.

Edwin scrambled back up the slippery little path and walked resolutely back towards the front entrance of the castle.

From a distance he could see a crowd milling round the gate house. Before he even reached the gate, to his amazement people were coming forward to greet him. Word seemed to have spread outside the walls of his surprise escape from Lord Peverell's champion archer and everybody wanted to congratulate him.

People were clapping him on the back, hugging him, ruffling up his hair, and those who couldn't get close enough to touch him were calling out and whistling after him.

He was swept up by the press of people and found himself carried away from the gate to an open, flat grassy area.

A man pushed forward to Edwin's side. He was young, quietly-spoken and smiling. His wife and three small, bouncy children crowded behind him.

"I'm Ingold and this is my wife, Deva. We would like you to come and join us. We've brought a picnic and you're more than welcome to share it."

At the mention of food, Edwin suddenly realised he was famished, and a meal seemed like a very good idea.

Edwin let himself be led along as they detached themselves from the crowd and made off towards the shelter of a big tree.

"Sit you down here, my duck." Deva gathered her brood around her and pulled Edwin down beside her as the children settled themselves at her feet.

Ingold put down a sack he was carrying and started to empty it. There was fruit and cheese and coarse, grey bread and a flagon of milk.

"Where are the hard boiled eggs and the rissoles. Didn't we pack them?"

Deva fussed round the children as Ingold delved into the sack and brought out yet more to eat.

Mother and father both handed round the food and the whole family began to eat, urging Edwin to do the same.

The children squabbled and fought over who would sit next to Edwin and finished up all taking a turn. They watched whatever he chose to eat, and then they took the same.

"We heard you kept your nerve in front of his lordship, lad," Ingold told him, through a mouthful of bread and cheese. "We're glad to see you out of there and holding your head up."

Deva smiled at him as she refilled his beaker of milk.

"Rissole?"

Edwin had no idea what he was being offered. The rissoles looked a bit like burgers but he wasn't sure what they'd taste like. To be polite he took one. Deva saw him studying it.

"They're bacon and mushroom."

That sounded reassuring. Edwin bit into his rissole. It was delicious. He accepted a second one.

He was amazed to find himself the hero of the day.

He wondered what he would be expected to do in exchange for his supper but the family made no demands on him. They only wanted to share their meal with him to show how glad they were that he had come out on top in an unequal contest. Saxon versus Norman. A Saxon winner was a rarity.

Eventually the picnic party broke up. It was time for Ingold and Deva to take their children home to bed. At first they tried to persuade Edwin go with them, but he assured them he would be okay on his own.

There were a couple of rissoles left over and Deva insisted he take them with him for later.

He stowed them carefully in his shoulder bag. He would make sure Granny didn't starve.

Edwin thanked them for their kindness and hospitality and gave each of the children a hug goodbye.

Daylight was draining away into dusk. People were wending their way home across the grass. Now Edwin's first problem was to get back in through the gates.

Luck was with him again. The gate keeper was involved in a noisy exchange with a group of workmen who were moving some large panels through the entrance. They'd dropped one and it had landed on the slant, blocking the way.

None of the men was watching the gateway – they were too busy arguing. Edwin crouched down and darted under the half-fallen panel.

So, he was back inside. Now he had to locate Granny in the big, sprawling complex of buildings and alleyways that made up the castle.

How could he possibly find her? Where to start?

The simplest thing would be to go up to a soldier on guard and ask him where she was. That was also the simplest way to find himself straight back in prison. No, he had to do this without giving away what his intention was. Look for her without anyone realising that was what he was doing. How on earth could he do that?

Think, Edwin, think.

The only thing he could come up with was to go round yelling "Granny" at the top of his voice and see if she answered. But that was a dead give-away, wasn't it? He might try it once but as soon as one of the soldiers heard him he'd lose any opportunity for a second attempt.

No, he had to be more subtle than that.

He had to think of some way to let her know he was trying to find her without anyone else cottoning on to what he was doing.

Five more minutes of solid thinking and he'd got it. Blondie! Wasn't that the name of that minstrel who had sung a song under the castle windows and waited for a voice to join in the chorus? That was it.

If he went round singing his head off, anyone who heard him would think he was mad, but they all thought he was a nut-case anyway, so what did it matter.

Problem was, what to sing. What song did he know that Granny would know the chorus to? That was easy. There weren't any. The songs he knew didn't have choruses.

He could try the national anthem, they'd both know that. But it might be a dodgy choice in his present circumstances. He had no idea who had written it, or when, and he didn't want to find out the hard way that it was by a composer who sympathised with the Saxons.

He'd never heard Granny sing so he hadn't the faintest idea what sort of music she liked. What a problem!

Then he remembered. He had heard Granny singing. The egg boiling song! He'd teased her about it. How did it go? "I'm dreaming of a white Christmas." That was it!

It didn't matter whether he got the tune right or not, Granny would recognise it. And if the locals heard him singing about Christmas in the middle of summer, well, that would just confirm to them that he was completely mental.

# CHAPTER 17

"I'm dreaming of a whi-i-i-i-te Christmas!" Edwin bawled his head off for the fiftieth time, this time at the corner of a blind alley on the furthest side of the castle from the gate house.

He'd tried to be methodical and work his way from one side to the other of the grounds, without missing anywhere out or going back to the same place twice. He'd sung until he was nearly hoarse but so far nobody had answered.

He'd got plenty of strange looks and at one point a little gaggle of cheeky lads had followed a few yards behind him, shouting their own version of what he was singing.

They'd got fed up and left him alone after a bit, but Edwin had doggedly worked his way past every battlement and parapet, determined not to give up until he got the response he was listening for.

He paused to draw breath and in that instant, he heard it:

"I'm dreaming of a white Christmas!" Only this time it was sung in tune.

"Gran!"

"Up here, Edwin!"

Far up in a turret at the top of a tower above the wall at the end of the alley, a hand was waving through the bars of a small window.

Edwin's heart sank. Gran was miles away. How could he possibly reach her up there?

"Come closer!" Gran's voice was clear on the night air. He ventured down the alley until he was as close as he could get to the high wooden wall. He noticed there was a small doorway, well set back in an alcove. He hoped nobody would come dashing out to see what all the noise was about.

Seconds later Edwin did a quick side-step as something came hurtling down from above. It hit the ground so hard that sparks flew up off the stones. He reached out to grab whatever it was and found his hand closing round Gran's Swiss Army knife.

He pulled his fingers away sharply as he realised one of the blades was sticking out. Perhaps it had come open in the fall, or when it hit the ground. He looked more closely. It was the accessory Gran had told him was the lock-pick. At the time, he had thought she was joking. Now, he hoped she hadn't been.

Here was a door. Here was a lock. Here was the pick. He set to work.

Edwin had never picked a lock before. He really had no idea what he was doing but it couldn't be that complicated, surely. Put the pick in the lock and wiggle it about until the door opened. That was the only strategy he had, so that was what he did.

Either the lock was a very simple one, or the pick was very efficient, or Edwin was very lucky. He really didn't care which. He was just very glad when he heard a metallic thunk and the door eased open under his cautious pressure.

He expected to feel a hand on his collar the moment he put his head round the door, but to his great relief there was no-one there. He slipped inside and pushed the door shut behind him without locking it again. This might be their only way out.

Keeping as quiet as he could, he crept forward. He was in a small, square entrance hall. A dim, spluttering lantern hung on the wall above his head. For a moment Edwin thought of taking it with him. He reached up to feel the weight of it and realised immediately he wouldn't be able to lift it up high enough to get it off its hook.

By its dull light he could make out the foot of a wooden staircase. It was wide enough for two people to pass each other and took up most of the available space in the hall. He looked up but the top of the staircase disappeared into darkness. It was dead quiet.

He still had the Swiss Army knife in his hand, with the lock-pick accessory out. He closed it up and was about to stow it in his shoulder bag when he had a second thought. He opened the largest blade. Then, stepping as lightly as he could, with the knife held out in front of him, Edwin started to climb the stairs.

He hardly dared breathe as he mounted higher and higher. He was alert for the slightest sound. At every turn of the stairs he expected someone to be coming down in the opposite direction.

But no-one disturbed him as he went up one flight after another, clinging on to the rough wooden hand rail with one hand and keeping his knife held out ahead of him with the other.

He must be climbing up the tower. Every little while, at the turn of the stair, another lantern threw out a weak gleam. They didn't give enough light to see anything in detail but Edwin was very grateful not to be in going up in complete darkness.

At each landing on the staircase where a lantern hung, he could make out a doorway which he guessed must lead off into the main part of the building. In that case, there must be other ways in and out. Edwin crossed his fingers that most people went the other way and not up the tower.

The steps were steep and there were hundreds of them. He had to stop several times to catch his breath. He wondered how long it had taken Gran to climb all this way up.

As he was resting by the wall, well away from the light of the nearest lamp, he heard voices. He stiffened and pressed himself back into the woodwork. But the voices didn't come any nearer. He strained his ears but couldn't catch individual voices, just a dull drone of conversation beyond the door.

It was quite late. Perhaps the door led to a dining room where people were sitting down to their evening meal. He hoped they would be more interested in what they were eating than investigating an intruder on the stairs. He carried on up.

Without warning, the stairs opened up into a room. Edwin quickly bobbed back down below floor level and held his breath until he was sure there was no-one there.

He crept back up the last few steps into a square room with window openings and another lantern, this time hanging down from the middle of the ceiling. A quick glance round showed no doorways opening off. Edwin reckoned for the moment he was safe, so he took the opportunity to flop down and stretch his legs out in front of him.

He peered out of the nearest gap in the wall. He could see a lot of little lights not far below. It must be a swarm of fireflies. Amazing. He'd never seen fireflies before. But as he looked, he realised they weren't moving at all. They weren't insects. Those pin-pricks of light must be campfires and so that must be the ground down there. Had he really climbed so high?

How much higher was Granny? He stood up and looked round the room. What was that in the far corner? He went carefully over to investigate. There was a narrow opening into a vertical shaft. It seemed the only way up from there was by spiral staircase. He took a deep breath and set his foot on the first rung.

He climbed into total darkness. The people in the tower weren't going to waste their lanterns. It wasn't like any jailers were going to be visiting. Once locked in, Granny was supposed to be left there to die, so why would they bother lighting the stairs. Edwin's blood boiled with anger.

He climbed as fast as he could, but after once or twice missing his footing, he slowed down and went more carefully. It was bad enough that each tread got narrower towards the middle, but the stairs were broken and uneven, too. There was no hand-rail here, not even a rope by the wall. If he slipped, there was nothing to grab, nothing to stop him falling right back to the bottom of the spiral.

Edwin finally reached the top, panting for breath. The door to Granny's prison was right across the top step.

Granny must have heard him on the way up:

"Edwin? Is that you?"

He was so glad to hear her voice.

"Yes, Gran. I'm here. Just let me get my breath back and I'll get you out."

He sat down one step from the top and gulped down some air. The only thing he could find to cling on to was the underside of the step he was sitting on. Working one-handed, he closed the blade on the Swiss Army knife and re-opened the lock-pick tool. Then he stood up and braced himself as firmly as he could, ready to tackle the lock.

He reached out and touched the door ahead of him, moving his hands carefully over the surface.

He found a hinge, low down on the left side. So the lock must be on the right. He moved his hands up and down the rough wood, his fingers searching for the lock. It might be either a metal plate or simply a hole in the wood.

He didn't care what it was, just as long as he found it soon.

But however hard he searched, he couldn't find the lock. He couldn't believe it. He started to panic.

"Gran. I can't find the lock. Can you find it on your side and tell me where to look. Only it's pitch dark out here."

"I don't think there is a lock, Edwin."

"What?"

No lock on a prison door? There had to be.

"They didn't open the door with a key. They had to move a bar out of the way to get in, so I guess they put it back when they left."

"Right. I'll look for a bar."

He had no idea what sort of a bar he was searching for. He just hoped he would know it when he found it.

Edwin edged himself up on to the very top step, balancing precariously, and slid his hands slowly up the door as high as he could.

About level with his head, his hands collided with a big, solid, heavy beam of timber. It stretched right across the door and dropped into two iron-clad slots in the woodwork on either side.

Whoever had put in the bar in place was much taller than Edwin. And it had taken two of them, to position it on both sides of the door so that it dropped down evenly into its slots. Nobody could possibly open the door from inside.

Edwin's great fear was that he wasn't going to be able to open it from the outside, either.

# CHAPTER 18

Edwin took his sacking socks off so he could get a better grip with the rubber soles of his trainers. He got himself into position on the top stair. He stood with his feet wide apart, one on either side of the step, braced against the wall.

In the darkness he couldn't see what he was doing but that was no problem. He knew where the bar was. He knew what he had to do with it. He knew how heavy it was. He knew it was a lost cause.

And yet, what else could he do? He hadn't told Gran how hopeless it was. Only that it looked as though it might be difficult, but he would try.

He stretched his arms up until he could feel the bar. He grasped it firmly with both hands, took a deep breath and heaved upwards with all his might. The bar moved, he shifted his feet a little to get more purchase, then strained at it again as hard as he could. There was another slight movement, but the moment he relaxed his muscles the bar dropped back.

He whipped his fingers out of the way to avoid getting them crushed, then shook his hands to get the feeling back into them. He moved his feet to the middle of the step to take the tension out of his ankles.

He took a short breather, then got back in position and tried again. Again he was thrown back as the bar slammed back into its slots.

Undeterred, he went at it again. And again. Granny was behind that door. He was not going to let it beat him.

He couldn't get any higher up the door. The top step ran out where the door began and there was no purchase whatever on the wood of the door itself. If he scrambled up that far, he would have nothing to hold on to. If he slipped, there was only a long drop behind him, back to the foot of the spiral staircase.

But still, he did it. He threw himself at the door, grasping at the iron slot on the left side and dragging himself up by it. He balanced precariously, grateful for the darkness so that he couldn't see the void below him.

"This is it, Gran. I'm in a better position this time. I might be able to lift it."

"Be careful, Edwin. I don't want you to hurt yourself."

"Don't worry about me, Gran."

He grasped the slab of wood and willed all his muscles to work together to shift it. After an agonisingly long moment it moved, sliding upwards, juddering against its restraints.

"Yes!"

In the moment that victory seemed to be his, Edwin lost his balance. The bar thudded back into place, and Edwin fell, bumping and bouncing down the shaft until he landed, winded, in a heap at the bottom.

When he revived sufficiently to sit up, Edwin's first thought was Gran.

"I'm okay, Gran! I'm at the bottom of the stairs. Don't worry."

Then he crawled out into the room at the foot of the spiral staircase and flopped out as close as he could to one of the window gaps. The fresh air helped. Little by little, he calmed down, although for a while he was too shaken to move.

He stuck out one limb at a time, checking to feel if anything seemed to be broken. Miraculously, it felt as though he had got away without serious injury. Still, he had to sit for a while before he could risk standing up. When he did, his head swam and he had to steady himself against the wall. Negotiating more stairs definitely didn't seem like a good idea.

But what else could he do? He had to face the fact he wouldn't be able to move the bar on his own. He would have to go down the stairs and try to get help. Mad though it seemed, he couldn't think of any other way. The place might be full of soldiers, he might get re-arrested and thrown back into jail for trying to rescue a condemned prisoner, but there was just a hundred-to-one chance that he would come across someone who would be willing to help him. It was the only chance they had, so he had to take it.

Before he went down, he gritted his teeth and went up the spiral staircase again to tell Gran what he intended to do.

"Gran?"

"Oh, Edwin, I'm so glad to hear you. You frightened me to death when you fell down the stairs."

"Sorry about that. But I'm okay."

"That's good."

"Only, I can't open the door by myself, Gran. I'm just not tall enough. So I'm going to go back down and see if I can find someone who'll help me."

"Edwin! Have you gone mad!"

"I know, I know, Gran. It sounds daft. But it's the only way. I promise I'll be careful. I'll keep out of the way of the soldiers. It might take a while. But I'm sure there's someone here around this castle who will be willing to come back with me. Just be patient. I promise I'll be back."

"No rush, Edwin. I'm not going anywhere."

Going much more slowly this time, Edwin retraced his steps, backing down the spiral staircase and then setting off down the main flight.

He flicked open the blade of the Swiss Army knife again and carried it at the ready. He didn't know if he would dare to use it, but it gave him courage to have it in his hand. He was very relieved that the staircase was as deserted as it had been on his way up.

He was not many flights down when a slight sound caught his ear. He stopped instantly, all senses alert, and listened as hard as he could. There it was again. It sounded like somebody crying. Yes, definitely. That's what it was. Someone sobbing.

Well, that was probably a girl so maybe he wouldn't face a sword or a spear in his face if he crept in on her. He tiptoed down to the next landing and saw a door. He pushed at it gingerly and it opened on to a passageway. The heart-rending sobs were coming from very nearby. He could see no door, but a heavy tapestry hung over an opening in the passageway wall.

Edwin moved silently over to the tapestry and tweaked the side of it back to peep into the room beyond.

The chamber looked comfortable and well furnished. There were more tapestries on the walls. There were two big, comfortable chairs with woven throws and cushions, several side tables, and a polished wood cupboard. There was a large wooden chest with a tray of drinking goblets and a flagon on it. The room was lit by fat yellow candles burning in several floor-standing, metal holders.

Curled up in one of the chairs, with her back to Edwin, was the young woman who was crying. Her long blond hair fell round her shoulders and her face was buried in her hands as she wailed and wept inconsolably.

She might not be the best help he could hope for but she was his only hope, so Edwin slipped past the tapestry and into the room.

"H-hmm . . ." He cleared his throat, hoping to attract her attention.

She didn't hear him. She seemed lost in a world of her own, drowned in her sorrows.

"Excuse me . . ." Still she didn't respond. Edwin tried again, a little louder:

"Excuse me . . ."

This time the figure in the chair reacted. She turned to face him, face wet with tears and lips still trembling.

But instead of a hysterical young woman in the chair, Edwin realised he was confronting a distraught young man.

They stared at each other, completely taken aback. The young man jumped to his feet:

"Who are you?"

Edwin's mind raced. Without knowing why he did it, he dropped to one knee in front of the blond youth.

"My name is Edwin. I mean you no harm."

The young man stared at him. Edwin realised what a sorry sight he must be, a rag-bag of crumpled clothing, and covered in cuts and bruises.

For a moment the silence held between them. Then the blond youth spoke. He had a soft voice but it was husky from crying.

"I know you. You are the boy who escaped the bowman this afternoon."

"That's right."

"I recognised you from yesterday. You were at the camp, weren't you?"

Edwin nodded, puzzled. How could this young man possibly know that?

"I heard you speaking with a woman, outside Ralf Giffard's tent. You said you were going to find my wife and baby and bring them back to me."

What! Edwin couldn't believe it. Entirely by accident, he had stumbled upon the real Lord Kinmer!

He was so young. He couldn't be more than seventeen, perhaps eighteen at the very most. He was slim and fine-boned and as blond as any Saxon. Yet he was a Norman lord. Lord of the manor, in fact. It didn't seem possible.

Edwin forced himself to stay calm.

"Yes, my lord. That's right. I was with my grandmother. We didn't see you."

"I came out from my tent but you ran away before I could speak to you."

"We heard somebody coming. We didn't know who it was."

Again the silence between them.

Edwin couldn't take his eyes from Kinmer.

"We will do everything we can to help you, my lord."

Kinmer looked back long and hard at Edwin, then he smiled and it changed his face completely.

"I hope I can trust you. You bear my mark, which gives me confidence in you."

What was he talking about? Edwin had no idea. He had no response but to smile back.

Then to his amazement Kinmer pointed to the logo on Edwin's trainer.

"The one-winged bird. My son bears a birth-mark just like this on his right shoulder. I have adopted it as my sign. If you wear my sign, I believe I can trust you."

"My lord, I am your man. And my Gran wears your sign too. I promise you can trust us, me and my Gran."

"She was condemned by Lord Peverell."

Edwin lowered his eyes.

"I know. Only she hasn't done anything wrong. It was all a mistake. Please believe me. We were nothing to do with any plot. Gran's all I've got in the world. She's innocent. She's locked up at the top of this tower. I've been trying to get her out of there but I can't open the door by myself."

Even as he said the words, Edwin knew they were hopeless. Kinmer would never believe him.

"You vowed to restore my family to me. I will do what I can to reunite you with your family. I believed in your grandmother's innocence when she spoke at her trial. I may incur the wrath of Lord Peverell for freeing one of his prisoners, but that is a risk I will take."

"Oh, my lord, if you can help me rescue her, I promise we'll try and help you get your wife and son back."

Kinmer smiled. Now he had something to do, he looked much happier.

"I could send for some of my men to help but my heart tells me this is a venture best kept entirely private between us."

"Thank you, my lord."

"Lead the way, Edwin, and I will do what I can."

"It's dark up in the turret, sir."

Kinmer nodded. He opened the cupboard and took out a couple of small metal lanterns with candles inside. He lit them from one of the bigger candles burning in the holders and passed one to Edwin and held the other aloft.

"Ali vuzon, Edwin."

"Wee-wee, my lord," Edwin replied, with a big grin.

# CHAPTER 19

Kinmer went ahead up the cramped staircase and located hooks to hang the lanterns on. Then, they were able to see hand and foot holds which must have been for the soldiers' use, which Edwin had missed in the darkness.

Edwin squeezed past Kinmer, on to the top step, and called through the door:

"It's me, Gran. I told you I'd come back."

"You were quick. I didn't expect you for another couple of days. Who's with you?"

"Lord Kinmer, Gran."

"What?"

"It's lucky he's so thin, otherwise he'd never be able to get up this rat-hole. And he's so tall he'll easily be able to lift the bar out of its sockets."

Edwin hoped desperately that Gran would pick up his clues and realise that the man outside the door was not the Kinmer they thought they'd seen at the camp.

"And Gran, another thing . . ."

"Yes?"

"Better taking the sacking off your feet. You'll have a better grip on the stairs. It was really helpful to me that I'd done that."

Lord Kinmer needed to see she wore the mark that meant so much to him.

"Please tell me you'll do that, Gran?"

"All right, Edwin. I'm sure you know best." Gran's voice was cautious.

He crossed his fingers and hoped that she had read a second message in his instructions.

He was half afraid of what they would find when the door swung open. Although he had spoken to Gran, he would not be happy until he saw her. Was she really okay? Had the soldiers hurt her at all? Had she been so exhausted by the long climb up the stairs they would have to carry her down?

Edwin backed carefully past Kinmer, on to a lower stair. Kinmer stepped up to the door and placed his feet firmly in the footholds. He rolled up his sleeves, grasped the bar, flexed his muscles and heaved. The effort made him grunt but the bar moved smoothly and evenly up out of its two sockets.

As soon as the bar was free, Kinmer swung it round at an angle so that it wedged itself between the walls. Then he braced himself against it as he kicked the door open.

Edwin could have jumped for joy to see Granny standing upright by the door, her shoulder bag and shawl gathered to her, ready to leave. She bobbed her head to Kinmer.

"Thank you very much, I'm sure."

If Gran was surprised to see who her rescuer was, she gave no hint of it. Edwin couldn't suppress a grin. Gran's acting was star quality.

Kinmer gave Gran his hand and helped her edge past him onto the top step. Edwin led the way, backing carefully down the perilous stairs. Gran followed and Kinmer came last with the lanterns.

"Take your time, good mother."

Gran took his advice.

At last they were down in the little square room where the staircase proper began. They took a moment's break there and when they continued their descent, Kinmer led the way.

They had less reason to fear encountering the soldiers with Kinmer to vouch for them, but still they were glad that the staircase remained deserted.

"I will take you back to my chamber. We need to talk."

With a jolt, Edwin realised Kinmer was expecting them to outline a plan to rescue his wife and child. He had assured Kinmer that's what they were going to do. But that was when they thought Stan was holding them in the caves. Now, they had no idea where they were. They actually couldn't promise Kinmer anything at all.

Edwin felt hot and cold all over. Would Kinmer think Edwin had lied to him, just to secure Gran's release? How angry would he be?

All Edwin could do was cross his fingers and hope that Gran would think of something fast.

Kinmer's first concern, when they got back to his room, was to look after Gran. He settled her in the most comfortable chair with a rug around her knees. Edwin sat on a cushion on the floor at her feet. Gran shook the rug out and tucked one corner round Edwin's shoulders.

Kinmer crossed to the chest and lifted the flagon. Satisfied it had plenty in it, he poured a drink for each of them and brought them across. Then he sat down in the chair opposite Gran. He raised his goblet:

"To liberty!"

"To liberty!"

"To liberty!"

The drink was delicious. It was a clear, golden colour, slightly sweet and Edwin thought, probably alcoholic. It slipped down.

Gran did her best to smother a hiccup.

"The mead is very good, my lord, but I'd better not drink much. I've had nothing to eat all day."

"Gran!" Edwin was mortified to have forgotten.

Kinmer was on his feet in a moment, full of apologies, too.

"I should have thought. I may have something here I can offer you."

Edwin fumbled in his shoulder bag and produced the wreckage of the rissoles.

"Sorry. I think I must have landed on my shoulder bag when I fell down the stairs."

"I'll manage nicely with those bits of rissole, if I can just have a plate, please."

Kinmer fetched a plate from the cupboard. Edwin put the fragments of rissole on it and handed it to Gran.

"Hmm . . . very nice. Bacon and mushroom. Who made these? I'll have to ask for the recipe."

Kinmer watched in astonished silence as Gran demolished the heap of rissole crumbs in double quick time and washed them down with another good swig of mead.

"Do excuse me, young man. But there's nothing like being under sentence of starvation to sharpen the appetite."

Kinmer laughed out loud.

Granny didn't look at Kinmer. Her voice softened.

"I dare say it's the first time you've done that for a while?"

Edwin wondered if she guessed Kinmer's eyes would fill with tears again as soon as he was reminded of his loss.

"You've had a rough time of it lately, haven't you?" Gran's tone was gentle. "We don't come from these parts. Do you want to tell us about it?"

Kinmer took a gulp of mead. When he started to speak he kept his eyes fixed on the floor. His voice was hardly above a whisper.

"Bad times started when my father died at the beginning of the year."

"What happened?"

"He loved to hunt. He always considered it a great sport. He'd been a huntsman since he was a youth."

Kinmer paused for a long time. The story seemed to have dried up. Gran prompted him:

"Tell me about your father's growing up."

"He was called Kinmer, too. He was raised with Will Peverell. Life-long friends, they were. Knew each other from the cradle."

"William Peverell, the Governor here?"

"Yes. Will is the son of the king. He was born in Normandy when King William was about my age, long before he married Matilda of Flanders.

He wasn't allowed to marry Will's mother, although they say it was a love match. Her name was Inglerica, a young Anglo-Saxon noblewoman from London. But King William's marriage was arranged for political reasons, and Inglerica would be of no value in that regard.

After her son was born they married her off to a man named Peverell and later Will took his name.

"Baby Will's parents employed a nurse-maid, who raised him along with her own child. Will's nurse-maid was my grandmother. So my father and Will grew up together. They were close as brothers and their friendship lasted all the years.

"When Will was just turned twenty, he came to England and fought at his father's side at Hastings in 1066. My father was Will's chosen companion in that endeavour. After the victory, the king made Will a baron and Governor of Nottingham and this castle that they built here.

"Will, in turn, rewarded my father. He granted him a lea of land and made him lord of the Manor."

"Kinmers Lea."

"Yes. My father's family was not nobly born. He was the proudest man alive, to be given such an honour. He and Will Peverell thought the world of one another. But other things were not so good."

"What things?"

"The local people hated my father. The Saxons who had been dispossessed of their lands and their rights by the war would never accept their new landlord. He was a good man but he was a Norman.

That was enough for them. Their resentment knew no bounds.

"They seethe with bitterness still at the taxes they have to pay. But the local lords of the manor are not responsible. They may collect the dues but they don't set the rate of taxation, neither do they benefit from it.

King William's commissioners go about the land to survey and record the facts and figures. The king alone enjoys what goes into the coffers.

"I've heard tales of Azor and Grimkettle, Saxons who held that land before my father. They were not angels, either of them. Greedy and grasping and ready to offer 'protection' – for a fee! But they were Saxons.

So now, however much men complained about them before, now they speak of the 'good old days' before the Normans came.

"My father had a job to do, and he tried to do it fairly. But he was a Norman, so nothing he did could ever be right.

"He never stopped looking for ways to reconcile the Saxons to the new rule. My father took a Saxon wife. My mother – God rest her soul – was the daughter of his chief tenant. I'm half Saxon myself.

But still, they call after me 'Norman, go home!' I've never even been to Normandy. I was born in Kinmers Lea. I grew up there with the Saxons' own sons. Yet still they hate me and want to punish me."

Kinmer took a long drink of his mead and sat still for a while, trying to steady himself and control his feelings.

"What happened to your father?"

"They said it was a hunting accident. He had been hunting wild boar in the East Wood, not far away from home. My father never showed prejudice. There were Saxons as well as Normans in the hunting party. I was told a boar frightened his horse and it threw him.

He fell to the boar's tusks . . . although rumour has it that a Saxon dagger helped him on his way."

Edwin stiffened with shock.

Granny asked softly:

"What do you think happened?"

"I was loath to believe such a thing of any man. For a long time I told myself it was nothing but wicked tongues wagging. Yet now, I am not so sure.

"Since Edith and Robert disappeared, I fear an evil hand at work against my family. My father was a good and fair man. My wife and child have done no harm to anyone.

"Anger drives these Saxons. Do they not think of the anger they stir in me?"

# CHAPTER 20

Kinmer took another sip of mead and continued.

"I knew they resented my father but I always believed he had their respect, however grudging. Since his death I've learned just how much they despise me.

"I hear every taunt and jibe you can imagine. Never to my face, you understand. But whispered behind trees and hedgerows, repeated in the servants' quarters, gossiped up and down the manor. They even say they won't serve a half-Norman overlord. My father's Norman-ness was too much for them, now mine's too little!"

Kinmer gave a bitter laugh. He let his head rest back on the cushions and closed his eyes.

"Tell me about Edith."

"Ah . . . she is the sweetest thing!" Kinmer sat up and his expression changed. "She was always the only girl for me. I've known her since we were children." He fell silent again.

"Is she Saxon?"

"Oh, yes. She's the eldest daughter of my father's — that is to say, my household steward. Her younger brother is no older than you." He smiled at Edwin. "So, you see, our child is only one quarter Norman. How little of the wrong blood it needs to drive someone to such a vile deed."

At that, Kinmer lost his composure.

"My little boy is only two months old. I don't suppose I shall ever see my darlings again."

He bent forward, buried his face in his hands, and wept.

Edwin squirmed uncomfortably at the display of such raw emotions. Granny sat quietly and made no attempt to comfort Kinmer. At length, he gave a great, shuddering sob, sat upright again, wiped his face with the back of his hands, sniffed and bit his lip until he had himself under control again.

He smiled a watery smile at Granny.

"Edwin tells me you have a plan for their rescue. If this is true, please tell me now."

"I can make you no promises, Lord Kinmer, but I will tell you as much as I can. Edwin and I overheard some people talking about taking away your wife and child. At that time we had no idea when they intended to do this, or where they intended to take them.

"We followed them to the camp at Tilkington and there we learned that the deed had already been done. We also learned that the original plan was to bring them here, to Nottingham, and hide them in the caves under this very castle."

Kinmer sat bolt upright in his chair and his mouth dropped open in amazement. Before he could speak or stand, Granny held up a hand and quickly continued.

"However, we know the plan was changed at the last minute. You may be sure, my lord, they are not here."

Kinmer flopped back against the cushions.

"So where are they?"

Edwin dreaded Granny saying: "I don't know."

Her reply surprised him:

"I've been giving a good deal of thought to that, my lord. Having nothing else to do, in the absence of any company or any mealtimes to break the monotony upstairs.

"It seems to me there is, as you surmise, a vendetta against your family. I don't know if the rumour about your father's death is true, but you are right to think that the people who are spreading the rumour are confident it will be believed by some. There is no doubt about an anti-Kinmer faction in your locality."

Kinmer seemed relieved that his account had been believed. He sat forward. He wanted to hear what else Granny had to say.

"My lord. I think your wife and child are held captive in Kinmers Lea."

"What!"

"And I believe I know the house where the kidnapper has hidden them. It has already been visited by the soldiers and is now standing empty, while the tenants are otherwise occupied in the market square, on Lord Peverell's orders."

"The cottage, Gran! He's taken them to the cottage!" Edwin was up on his feet.

"It's his best bet. Nobody will go looking there again. It's already been searched once and nothing found. Garth and Arnie are not coming back, nor Wiglaf and Fred. Stan has the place to himself.

"Remember, Edwin, at the camp, Bebba said a man had been seen lurking nearby with a horse? Not a pair of horses, but a horse. He didn't take them away by cart. He rode, with Edith on the horse behind him, and no doubt Stan himself carrying the baby so that she wouldn't jump off and run away to give the alarm.

"That's why we didn't meet him on the road to Tilkington, coming the other way. He had no need to travel by road. He would have gone over the fields and through the woods. I'd bet a pound to a pinch of mouse dirt they've been in the house practically ever since we left it!"

By now they were all three up on their feet, Kinmer pacing, Gran checking the contents of her shoulder bag, Edwin hopping up and down from one foot to the other with excitement.

"Are we going after him, Gran?"

"Indeed, we are. Right now."

"What? How can you and the boy get from here to Kinmers Lea at this time of night?"

"We know where there's an ox cart with two good beasts that I'm sure will know their own way home at any hour of the twenty-four. You arm yourself, my lord, and bring a posse of men along with you at daybreak to Garth and Arnulf's cottage."

Kinmer protested:

"But those are the men charged with plotting against Lord Peverell. They made no denial of it at their trial. That is why they were found guilty and sent to hang."

"They didn't deny it because their only defence could be that their plot was against you instead! They would hang whichever plot they admitted to. But because the name of Kinmer was never mentioned, no-one made the connection between them and the disappearance of your family."

Kinmer threw himself down in the chair again.

"I knew those men well. We were neighbours. They worked my father's land – my land. I was shocked when I heard they'd been convicted of some wicked conspiracy against Lord Peverell. They didn't seem the type to deal in terror and death. And now I find I was their target. And they will go to the gallows in silence to spite me. How much do they hate me?"

Kinmer got up and poured himself another goblet of mead. He only took a sip before he subsided into the chair once more, his hand shaking. He was finding it hard to keep his composure when he turned to Granny again:

"What have they done to Edith and our baby?"

"That, we shall only know when we get to Kinmers Lea. You organise some back-up, my lord, and meet us there at daybreak. Edwin and I are setting off now."

# CHAPTER 21

Before they left, Kinmer did his best to persuade Gran to let him send one of his retainers with them.

"I'm not happy to let you set out unescorted. Are you sure you don't mind travelling in the dark? Will you be able to manage the cart and the beasts? What will you do if you meet rogues or vagabonds along the way?"

"You're making too much fuss, my lord. We shall manage just fine."

"Even if you are not prey to robbers, you may meet other dangers. Your route follows the open road through woods and moors as well as villages and hamlets."

"No-one will trouble with us, an old woman and a child. We've nothing of value."

"Wait a moment while I fetch some things I think you should take."

Before Granny could protest Kinmer had slipped out past the tapestry.

When he came back he was carrying two poles with curved hooks on the top, like shepherds' crooks. The hooks curved up again at the end and on one there hung a small lantern, like the ones they had taken up the spiral staircase, and on the other an open-work metal box of a similar size containing glowing embers of charcoal.

"Please don't refuse to take these. I should not be happy if you set out without light and fire. Take these extra candles and lumps of charcoal too, so you have sufficient to last through the night."

Their shoulder bags were bulging, but Kinmer insisted they manage to make room for some oat cakes and a small flagon of milk which he had found in his cupboard.

"Follow the main road out of the city to the north. When you come to the fork, bear right and continue without leaving that road."

Granny nodded.

"We shall be fine, my lord. Don't you worry about us. But what are you going to do now? It seems to me, begging your pardon, sir, that it wouldn't do you any harm to get a few hours sleep."

Kinmer smiled.

"You're right. I haven't closed my eyes since they went missing. But my heart is not yet easy enough for me to sleep. Time for that when Edith and Robert are found.

"First of all, I must speak with William Peverell. He is my liege lord and I am in duty bound to let him know the turn things have taken. There are also people here in this stronghold whose first allegiance is to me. They wear my sign, as you do." Kinmer smiled and glanced down at their feet.

"I must go around the castle and seek them out. We shall need arms and horses. Then we will ride to Kinmers Lea and meet you at the cottage at daybreak."

"We'll be off then."

Gran hoisted up her shoulder bag and crook. Kinmer stepped forward and held the tapestry open for them.

He bowed solemnly to Gran and she dropped a curtsey to him. Edwin was impressed. Gran wasn't play-acting this time. Kinmer bowed to Edwin, in turn, and Edwin straightened his shoulders and returned the compliment.

The long climb down the stairs was uneventful. The door at the bottom stood unlocked, just as Edwin had left it.

Gran blew out the candle in the lantern. They slipped out in utter darkness and crept towards the castle gates, keeping close to the walls and, where a light glowed in a window, dodging between the shadows.

The gate keeper was fast asleep in his cabin, snoring his head off. They sneaked past as fast as they could, grateful that he didn't keep a guard dog with him.

Once safely beyond the castle walls, Gran used the charcoal embers to light their little lamp again.

They needed Gran's sense of direction to guide them back to where Garth had left the cart. Edwin would have taken a wrong turn at every corner.

"Use your nose, Edwin!"

They were soon picking their way through the cowpats on the parking lot.

In a far corner they found Sunshine and Flower. They had been unhitched from the cart and stood side by side, tethered loosely to the cart by a rope round their horns, placidly chewing.

Gran went up and rubbed their noses.

"Sorry it's not your boss. You'll have to put up with a couple of amateurs in the driving seat tonight."

Edwin looked round.

"Where's their harness, Gran?"

"Have you tried looking on the cart?"

"Yes. It's not there."

The cart was parked, tipping forwards, resting on its long, single shaft. Edwin found the oxen's yoke over the end of the shaft, weighting it down.

"Got it, Gran."

"Good lad. Bring it over here and let's see how it fits."

Edwin stooped to lift the yoke and found himself experiencing the same problem as he had met outside Gran's prison door. The timber yoke, which was as tall as himself, was far too heavy for him to lift.

He stood up and said a very rude word under his breath. He had watched Garth pick that yoke up and carry it without any apparent effort.

"Gonna need a bit of help here, Gran."

With a great deal of pushing and shoving, between them they managed to move the yoke off the shaft. Immediately, the shaft began to rise as the tail-board of the cart dipped and everything slid to the back and off into the dirt.

Flower and Sunshine flicked their ears and carried on chewing.

"Amateurs was the word I used, wasn't it, Edwin? And I was right. I think we'd better wake up one of the parking attendants and give him the price of a good drink to get us on our way."

The surly youth who came to help them made no secret of his disdain for their efforts.

"'Ere, are you sure this ox cart actually belongs to you?"

"We're looking after it for the owners. They've been unavoidably detained in town on business. Must get the cart back to their place by breakfast time."

"Seems a rum story to me. Why didn't they pay a proper carter to drive it back? 'Ere, pick those sacks up, will you?"

Edwin held the two crooks while Gran rescued the clutter of sacking and other odds and ends and piled it all back on the cart.

"Is there somewhere to fix these crooks on?"

"'Ere, there's a bracket for a lamp on either side, at the front. Ain't you never been on a cart before?"

"I'll have you know, we arrived on this cart, young man."

Edwin spotted the brackets. He climbed up on the cart and fixed the crook with the lantern in one and the crook with the box of charcoal in the other. Then he jumped down again and joined Gran, watching the youth harness up the beasts. He made light work of the heavy yoke and cart shaft.

"'Ere, can you get them out on to the road by yourselves, or do you want me to do that for you?"

"Yes, perhaps you'd better."

"Cost you another penny, then."

Gran scowled.

"All right."

The youth went up ahead of the oxen and turned back towards them, clicking his tongue and making little clucking noises to them. Walking half-backwards, using his hands and his voice, he encouraged the oxen to follow him. Flower and Sunshine started forward slowly and in an expert manoeuvre the youth turned the whole rig in a half-circle and led them out of the parking lot and on to the road.

"'Ere, one of you had best walk alongside them to start with."

The surly youth turned away across the parking lot, hands in his pockets, leaving Sunshine and Flower ambling down the road.

Gran hurried ahead to catch up with the oxen.

"You jump up on the driver's seat, Edwin. I'll join you in a minute."

Edwin did as he was told and immediately wished he hadn't. He felt more inadequate in the driver's seat of the ox cart than when he sat behind the wheel in his mum's car.

How did you steer, for a start? There weren't any reins.

He knew it wasn't any good looking for brakes. And how did you get them to start walking again, if they ever stopped?

He could kick himself. He'd sat on the back of this cart behind Garth for hours, and hadn't noticed a single thing he'd done. All Edwin could remember was that Garth used to croon to the oxen in a funny sing-song voice, and they'd done exactly what he wanted.

The oxen had got into a slow, steady stride. Granny let them walk ahead of her and as the cart drew level, she climbed up alongside Edwin on the driver's seat. It was wide enough for two with room to spare. She was panting as she sat down.

"How do you steer this thing, Gran?"

"I rather think it's done with the use of the whip. If you want to go left, you tap Flower on the rump with the whip and he'll pull away in his direction. If you want to go right, do it on Sunshine's side."

"Where's the whip?"

After a brief hunt they found it among the tangled heap of sacking. Edwin tried flicking it, but only managed to catch himself a stinging blow round the face.

He felt like a complete waste of space, sitting up there in the driver's seat as the oxen plodded along, totally regardless of anything he did. It was like being the conductor of an orchestra that was going to play its own tune whether the conductor waved his arms about or not.

"This is a nightmare, Gran. I haven't got a clue what I'm doing."

"Don't worry, Edwin. Just leave it to the oxen. The only time we need to be careful is when we come to the fork. Probably best then if I get down and walk with them to make sure we go the right way."

Two massive, single-minded, bone-headed, stubborn oxen with a pre-determined idea of which road they were going to take at the fork, and Gran trying to tell them otherwise.

There was only one way that was going to go. Gran's way.

# CHAPTER 22

The oxen made no difficulties about forking right and before long Edwin and Gran were settled down on the driver's bench, with their little lantern throwing a pool of pale light on to the road and the charcoal giving off an occasional spark within its cherry-red glow.

The first change to the regular pattern of the oxen's hooves was when they splashed through a stretch of water on the outskirts of a village.

"I think this must be Radsford."

"How do you know that?"

"Well, calling it 'ford' is a bit of a give-away. I know the road between Nottingham and Kinmers Lea. I'm assuming the direction of that road won't have changed much over the centuries. Why would it? By my reckoning, this is about where Radsford is."

It was a night of scudding clouds and intermittent beams of moonlight. Sometimes they could see quite clearly the houses and hedgerows as they trundled by. At other times they rode in almost total darkness, apart from the light of their lantern.

Sunshine and Flower plodded along and the cart swayed in the well-worn ruts. The crunching and grating of the wheels was the only noise for miles around. It sounded very loud in the stillness of the night.

"Don't they get tired, Granny?"

"Apparently not. They'd had a good rest back at the parking lot, so I don't think we need worry about giving them a breather. Besides, do you know how to stop them?"

"No."

"Neither do I!"

They both laughed.

Some miles on, the oxen waded through another stream and shortly afterwards the moon broke through to reveal an almost desolate landscape. There were no fields or farms or cottages to be seen.

Just a dead flat expanse of short, wiry turf which seemed to shine pearly-white in the moonlight.

"This must be White Moor."

"It's a good name for it. Why is it white?"

"It only looks white at night because of the moonlight. During the day I expect it's a muddy brown."

"Why does moonlight make it look white, Gran?"

"It makes everything look white. The moon doesn't actually give any light. What we're seeing is second-hand sunlight, reflected off the moon."

"But the sun's gone down, ages ago."

"It's all a matter of geometry, Edwin."

"What?"

"I dare say someone's mentioned geometry to you at school, Edwin, although by the look on your face you thought they were talking about some kind of citrus fruit. Geometry is arithmetic with angles.

"The sun is below the horizon and the moon is up there. Because of the angles, so far as the moon is concerned, the sun's still shining. The sunlight shines on the moon and because of the angle we're at down here, we see the sunlight reflected off the moon, on to us.

"Please don't ask me what those angles are, but trust me, Edwin, there are a lot of angles involved. And here is the moonlight to prove it."

"Is there such a thing as second-hand moonlight?"

"Yes."

"What's that called?"

"It's called a thump on the head for asking too many questions. Now, do you want a drink of milk?"

Gran still had the pottery mugs in her shoulder bag. She took the stopper out of the flagon and poured them both a drink. When they had finished she made sure the stopper was firmly back in place and packed everything away.

The cart rolled out of the moonlight and under the shade of over-arching trees. The little candle seemed to glow brighter as they entered a stretch of woodland.

Ahead, the road appeared to vanish into a dark tunnel. Looking back, Edward could see nothing at all behind them except the branches that flicked back and closed around the trunks as the cart passed by.

"Do you know where we are now, Gran?"

"Not exactly, but I've a good idea. Lord Kinmer said our road would carry us through woodland and this is the first we've seen. I assume we're pretty far out of the city now."

Sounds were different under the trees. Although the cart wheels were still loud, they seemed more muffled here. And it soon became apparent that they were not alone.

Although they couldn't see beyond the lamplight, they could hear rustling and snuffling all around them. Nocturnal forest creatures were out on their regular patrol, hunting for beetles and bugs in the undergrowth.

Edwin stared all around, as hard as he could, but there was nothing to be seen beyond the sides of the cart. He wondered what could be out there – foxes, maybe, badgers, rats, mice, shrews. It seemed really strange, being able to hear them but not see them. Half of him was glad, because he was scared of wild animals, but half of him was really, really curious about what was making all those noises.

One of the noises began to be more noticeable than the others. It was quite a loud coughing sort of grunt. He tried to imagine the animal at the other end of the sound effects. Not a fox. What sort of noise did badgers make? Before he could think too much about that, there was one, much louder snort and suddenly something tore out of the forest and smashed into the side of the cart.

It was such a heavy blow that the whole cart rocked. Edwin and Gran were thrown up against each other on the driver's seat, and then apart again, as the left-hand wheel was pushed up, then settled down again.

"What was . . . that?"

"It felt like a charging rhinoceros, although in this particular location I think it's doubtful that it actually was one."

"Where's it gone?"

A demented scrabbling and scuffling were their only clues. Whatever the creature was, it had clearly backed off after ramming into the cart. Their best hope was that it would not repeat the experiment.

Sunshine and Flower had clearly been unnerved by the collision. Their pace had faltered and gradually they slowed to a complete halt.

"Don't stop! Don't stop! Gran, how do I make them not stop? It might come back!"

Gran took up the whip and tried to encourage the oxen to move forward. But either her voice was too unfamiliar, or they were too upset by the impact, because nothing she did was successful in urging them forward.

Edwin was staring over the side of the cart when the animal charged again. It came thundering out of the undergrowth with the unstoppable momentum of a steam locomotive going for the world speed record. It slammed into the big, solid wheel of the cart and lifted it a couple of feet off the ground.

For a long moment, the cart hung suspended on one wheel, then slowly lurched back to earth. Edwin hung on like grim death, watching the infuriated creature on the ground below, with dreadful fascination.

It was the size of a small Shetland pony, but the shape of a pig. It's dark outline blurred into the shadowy undergrowth, making it seem larger and more menacing still. Its face was pointed, with small, beady eyes that gleamed with malice. Worst of all were the two fearsome tusks that protruded from its bottom jaw, that Edwin was sure were capable of upending the whole vehicle.

'He fell to the boar's tusks . . .'

The words flew round and round in Edwin's head. To fall off a horse in front of a beast like this, and be gored by those terrible fangs. That must have been what happened to Kinmer's father.

Looking at the crazed creature below him, Edwin wondered why anybody felt the need to add to the story by talking about using a dagger, when the thought of what those tusks could do made his stomach writhe.

"Gran . . . it's a wild boar!"

"Get the oxen moving!"

The only thing he could think of was to walk along in front of them and try to entice them to follow him, like the youth had done in the parking lot. He started forward.

"Edwin, no! Whatever you do, don't get off the cart!"

He turned back, to see Gran leaning over the side, staring down at the ravening monster below.

Edwin tried to think how Garth would cope in such circumstances. Well, he'd probably jump down, bash the boar over the head with his bare hands and take its tusks home for souvenirs.

"Quick, Edwin, pass me the charcoal burner!"

Edwin jumped to obey. His hands fumbled as he pulled the crook out of its bracket. He almost let the container fall off its hook as he reached across and tried to pass the crook to Gran.

She took it from him, steadied the swaying charcoal box, and made sure she had a firm foothold. Then she opened the lid, stretched the crook out over the side of the cart and shook the box so that the top layer of burning charcoal fell. It landed on the snout of the angry boar beneath.

The noise it made was horrendous. It was somewhere between a screech and a bellow. But it worked. The boar backed into the bushes and they heard it crashing away, roaring and squealing.

As Gran retrieved the crook, some of the embers dropped inside the cart. She quickly stamped them out before they set fire to the sacking.

Edwin had a sudden idea.

"Gran, give me the crook, quick!"

He grabbed the crook and pushed it as far out in front of the driver's seat as he could. The crook was heavy and he had trouble holding it, but he hung on. The firebox was about level with the oxen's tails, but it would have to do. He shook it and a handful of glowing charcoal fell out.

It was exactly the shock Flower and Sunshine needed. They leapt forward, as one, swishing their tails. They even managed to trot a few steps before subsiding into a faster-than-usual walk.

With a gasp of relief, Edwin replaced the crook in its bracket, grabbed the whip and did his best to make sure the oxen kept up their pace.

Meanwhile, there was a terrible commotion in the bushes. Small, angry hooves beat a tattoo on the ground as the boar psyched itself up for one final, life or death charge.

It erupted out of the undergrowth, head down, going for the cart in the exactly the same place as it had before. But the cart had moved forward, just enough. The boar charged right past the tail-board, brushing the woodwork with its bristles.

Edwin caught sight of the surprised expression on its face as it hurtled unstoppably across the road and imbedded its tusks in a tree. There was a startled fluttering as half-a-dozen birds, nesting in the top-most branches, were thrown from their perch.

On the driver's seat, Edwin and Granny clung on to each other, half-laughing half-crying with relief.

Up ahead, Sunshine and Flower resumed their usual sedate plod as if nothing had happened.

# CHAPTER 23

Edwin and Gran breathed a sigh of relief as the thick canopy of leaves overhead gradually thinned. At last, they were back in open country and were surprised at how light the sky looked, compared with the dense blackness of the forest.

"It must be nearly dawn. We can't be far from Kinmers Lea now."

They had their breakfast of oat cakes and milk as they went along. Gran took off her shoulder bag.

"I'm going to leave this stuff on the cart. I'll try and find some more sacks to cover up our trainers."

Gran held on to Edwin's shoulder as she climbed over into the body of the cart and began sorting through the jumble of bits and bobs.

Edwin sat hunched on the driver's seat, watching the oxen's broad backs moving rhythmically as they towed the cart along. He wondered what would happen to them, now Garth and Arnie were not coming back.

It was a shame about Garth. He'd been a kind, good hearted man who had saved Edwin's life twice over. Now he was dead, convicted of a crime he didn't commit. He probably wouldn't even have been involved in the kidnap plot if it hadn't been for his brother. Edwin would always remember the way he spoke to the oxen.

"Gran? Who does the cottage belong to now Garth and Arnie have gone?"

"It'll be part of Lord Kinmer's estate."

"Do you think he'd let us live there?"

"We could certainly ask him. Although he might need it for his next ox driver. Unless you'd fancy taking a few lessons and applying for the job?"

Edwin laughed.

"Some hopes!"

"Here you are, Edwin." Gran climbed back over on to the driver's seat. "Put your sacks on."

"Are you calling me a Saxon?"

Gran smiled.

"Would you mind if I did?"

"I don't know. They can be evil. I think I prefer the Normans. I feel really sorry for Lord Kinmer."

"One swallow doesn't make a summer, Edwin. I would guess Kinmer is a bit of a one-off among the Norman nobility. Most of them are probably more like Lord Peverell. He's not exactly what you'd call cuddly, is he?"

"No. He's scary."

"And remember, not all the Saxons have turned to violence and intimidation against the Normans. Most of them have kept their heads down and got on with earning a living, even if they don't like the new regime. You shouldn't judge them all by the likes of Stan. He's an extremist."

"Yeh. He's a real fanatic."

"He is. And we shall be catching up with him very shortly.

"So what's the plan?"

"First of all, we're not going to let him know we're at the cottage until we absolutely have to. He won't be expecting us, so let's keep the element of surprise on our side."

"But won't he know as soon as he sees the cart?"

"We have to hope he hears the cart before he sees it. Unless someone has passed this way in the night and told him the latest news from Nottingham, he'll expect it to be Arnie and Garth coming home. The longer he assumes that, the better for us.

"The oxen will take the cart into the yard by themselves and stop where they usually do. We need to jump off before they pull into the yard and nip round the back of the cow shed.

"When Stan realises Garth and Arnie haven't come indoors he'll probably go outside and investigate. Might shout out first, but of course he'll get no answer. We have to hope he'll spend a little while looking around the yard. That will give us time for a quick search of the house.

"Remember, Edwin, our mission is to rescue Edith and the baby. We're not looking for a fight with Stan. If we can avoid even setting eyes on him, so much the better. If we can locate Edith and Robert and get them out of the house, even if we only take them and hide them in the hen coop, that's what we're going to do.

"So no heroics. Stan will be a desperate man. He knows if he's caught, he'll hang, so he's got nothing to lose. If we can get Edith and the child out without confronting him, so much the better."

"But what if we can't?"

"Then leave it to me, Edwin. I'm a trained hostage negotiator. I used to be with the S.A.S. . . ."

"Was that before or after . . ."

"Don't be cheeky. Just keep your focus. Remember, we're not out to get Stan. We're out to free the hostages. Right?"

"Yes, Gran."

"Keep what you carry to a minimum. Leave everything you don't need on the cart. Be ready to duck and dodge and run for it when I tell you."

The cartwheels sounded thunderously loud as they crawled up the road towards the cottage. Surely, anyone inside would have heard them coming half a mile away.

They slipped down from the drivers' seat and crouched on the back of the tailboard, ready to drop to the ground as Flower and Sunshine made the turn into the yard. By the time the oxen brought the cart to a creaking halt, Edwin and Gran were well hidden behind the cowshed wall.

They peeped out into the garden. Edwin nearly died of shock when the rooster let out a multi-decibel "Cock-a-doodle-doooo!" at the very moment he stuck his head round the wall. When his heart had gone back into the proper place in his chest and he could draw breath without choking, he tried again.

The garden and house seemed to be deserted. For a horrible moment Edwin thought they might have got it wrong and there was nobody there. That Stan had taken the hostages somewhere else.

Then he heard a slight sound from very nearby, and a second, more distant, sound from the house. The second sound was a baby crying. The first sound got louder and more insistent. It was a muffled croak, like someone trying to speak through a mouthful of sawdust. Gran darted forward and peered through the nearest window of the cowshed.

"Quick, Edwin! Give me another leg up, like you did before. But gently!"

It was the same window where he had pitched Gran through a bit too violently before. This time, he was more careful and Gran landed safely on the straw under the window. She reached a hand back through the window hole for Edwin and he scrambled after her.

They could see a dim shape wriggling about in the straw on the far side of the stall. Gran went across and quickly removed a piece of dirty sacking that had been bound across the mouth of the figure on the floor.

"Shhhhhhh . . . It's all right, Edith. We've come from Kinmer. We're here to help you get home."

"Oh, thank God!"

Granny helped Edith sit up and rest back against the wall. Then she delved into her bloomers and got out the Swiss Army knife. The blade made short work of the bindings round Edith's ankles and wrists.

"He's got Robert . . . he's got him in the house. I can hear him, but he won't let me have him with me." Edith was sobbing and gasping.

"Shhhhhhh . . . It's all right. We're here to get him back for you. You just try to relax. Let me rub your ankles where they were tied, try to get the circulation back. Then you'll be able to stand up."

Granny took each of Edith's feet in her hands in turn and massaged the ankles where the coarse string had cut in and marked the flesh.

"This is Edwin. Kinmer tells us you've got a brother about his age. I'm Edwin's Gran. Now, you're going to be all right with us. We'll look after you."

Gran continued rubbing Edith's wrists and ankles, stroking her hair back out of her face, gently calming and reassuring her.

Edwin looked down at the slight, fair-haired girl sprawled in the straw. She couldn't be more than sixteen. Her simple dress was made of slightly better material than sacking but it could hardly be called finery. Now it was dirty and muddy and she had lost her shoes. There was nothing to single her out as the wife of the lord of the manor.

Edith looked back and forth between Edwin and Gran.

"What's the man's name?"

"Athelstan."

"Who is he?"

"He's the husband of the woman you employed as nurse-maid to Robert."

"What? Bebba? I can't believe that. Are you sure?"

"I am."

"But she's going to have a baby soon herself. She wouldn't . . ."

"I'm very sorry to tell you that the woman you trusted with your son was planted in that job for the purpose of kidnapping him."

Edith sat silent for a moment, digesting this shocking information.

"What do they want? Is it ransom? Do they hope Kinmer will give them money?"

"I think that was part of the plan. Certainly Bebba hoped to make money from it. But Athelstan's motive is more to do with settling old scores. He harbours a terrible grudge against Kinmer's father."

"What for? He was a good man."

"Just for being Norman, I'm afraid, Edith."

"But we can't change what we're born. Why hate others for what they were born?"

"You and your young lord are shining examples of a happy partnership between two people who could have been sworn enemies. I'm afraid there are others who won't ever accept that."

Edwin was certain that Stan would consider such collaboration with the enemy an unforgivable crime. While ever Edith and baby Robert were in Stan's clutches, they were in grave danger.

# CHAPTER 24

In the cottage, baby Robert started to cry again. Edith was almost crying herself, frantic to get to her child.

"Listen to me, Edith. You've got to stay here for the moment. It's really important that Athelstan doesn't suspect anything. If you suddenly appear in the house, he'll know there's someone else here. You couldn't have got out of this stable on your own.

"We're hoping he'll go out to look for his friends on the cart. While he's doing that, Edwin and I will run into the house and grab Robert and bring him back to you. Then we'll get out of here as fast as we can."

"Where will we go?"

"We don't need to go far. Kinmer's following us along the road from Nottingham with a party of soldiers. He'll be here soon."

"Gran, he's on the move!" Edwin had been keeping watch on the cottage. Stan's bulky silhouette had moved across the window space in the direction of the yard.

"Okay! Now! We'll go into the house while he's outside. Edith, you stay here! Edwin, come on! Out the window, quick! We'll cut across the garden. Save you having to squeeze past the cows again."

Edwin was greatly relieved to be outdoors.

They kept close to the wall and carefully skirted the muddy area round the well. It seemed even more slippery and treacherous than before.

They could hear Stan pacing in the yard as they dodged through the sacking in the doorway and into the smoky interior of the cottage.

The baby was nowhere to be seen.

"Quick – look for a likely hiding place. He might have put him in a cupboard or under the table."

But there was no sign of the child and not even a whimper to be heard.

"He must have taken him outside with him. Come on back into the garden, quickly, Edwin."

They ducked back through the sacking and at that moment there was a shriek and a yell.

Edith had been unable to contain herself. In her anxiety to see her child, she had left the stable and run after Stan, who was standing in the yard, by the cart.

To judge by the commotion, Edith had tried to grab Robert out of Stan's arms but he had pushed her down and now came bursting into the garden, holding the crying child out in front of him.

He stopped dead in his tracks when he caught sight of Gran and Edwin.

"Who in the name of the devil are you?"

"This is Edwin and I'm his Gran. Good day to you, Athelstan. We've no interest in your person or your property, but I'd be very glad if you would pass over the infant to me, and I will see that he's safely returned to his parents before any more harm is done."

Gran stepped up in front of Stan, holding her arms out from her sides to show that she was not holding a weapon of any sort. Edwin stayed where he was, rooted to the spot, not wanting to do anything that would deflect Stan's attention away from Gran.

For a moment Stan stood where he was without moving a muscle. Then he relaxed, drew Robert closer to his chest, and gave a short, barking laugh.

"Are you serious, old woman? How do you think I should hand this child over to you? Have you any idea how much trouble I've had to go to, to get him in the first place. I shall not hand him over until my purpose with him has been served."

"I believe it already has been. You've driven his parents nearly mad with anxiety. Your point is made. You are not a man to be trifled with. His parents will understand that. They will pay whatever ransom you ask. So you may as well let the child go now, as when his father gets here."

Stan shot a hasty look over his shoulder, as if he expected to see Lord Kinmer riding in at the gate at that moment. Reassured, when all he saw was the bedraggled form of Edith limping into the garden, Stan laughed again.

"I'm telling you, old dame, go to hell!"

"Listen to me, Althelstan. You've done the baby no harm. If you return him now, I'm sure Lord Kinmer will take that into account. Don't keep this going until the child gets hurt. That can only make matters worse."

"I don't know who you are, or how you got into my house, but I'm telling you now to get out and don't come back. This child is going nowhere except with me!"

Granny stepped back to join Edwin. She lowered her voice.

"See those buckets of water, near the well? When I give the signal kick them over and make them spill as far as you can. I want the yard to be a sea of mud."

Edwin had a sudden idea. He could remember seeing a coil of rope on the window sill in the cow shed. He shot off and grabbed it through the window.

In a moment he was back and fastened the rope to the stoutest branch of a nearby bush. He tied the other end round his waist. If he was going to produce a mud bath to up-end Stan, he needed to make sure he was securely anchored himself.

Granny, meanwhile, was talking soothingly to Stan again, trying to persuade him to give up the baby.

Stan backed off, shielding the child, as if he expected Granny to try to snatch him.

"Athelstan, don't worry. I won't try to take him from you. I just want to talk to you. To try to get you to see reason."

Granny smiled at Stan and kept talking quietly. She also kept moving towards him, changing her position so that as Stan backed away from her, he moved closer and closer to the well.

Granny continued to direct a flow of calming words at Stan, edging ever closer to him so that he backed off further and further.

"Now would be a good time, Edwin."

Over went the buckets! Water sloshed everywhere. The area round the hole in the ground became a swamp. Granny had stopped walking towards Stan just far enough away from the well to keep on solid ground, but Stan began to slip and slide.

As Edwin got his foot to another bucket and sent yet more water swirling under Stan's feet, the big man lost his balance went down on his bottom. He had hold of baby Robert in both hands, like a rag doll. The child was screaming.

Edwin was afraid Edith might try another rescue attempt but she was slumped against the house wall, apparently unable to move. Her face was a mask of horror as she watched her child's ordeal.

Stan was slipping steadily towards the mouth of the well. Edwin moved out of his reach. He didn't want Stan grabbing hold of him. He doubted the rope, or the bush, would be able to hold the pair of them if they both went down the well.

While ever Stan held on to baby Robert, he couldn't use his hands to save himself. Eventually, he was flat on his back, his feet wedged against the further side of the well's opening. It was all that saved him from falling in.

Edwin gave a tug on his rope to make sure it was secure. Then he slopped through the mud into a position behind Stan's head and dropped to his knees.

Stan began to slip again and, as a reflex action, stuck out his hand to save himself.

In that moment, Edwin pounced. He seized the squirming baby and wrestled him out of Stan's grasp.

Granny grabbed hold of the rope and pulled Edwin to safety. Next moment, she had Robert in her arms and rushed across the garden to restore him to his sobbing mother.

Stan, meanwhile, was trying frantically to get a grip in the sea of sludge. He had already bent his knees and crooked up his legs into the mouth of the well in a desperate effort not to slide any further. In the end, it was only his bulk that stopped him dropping feet first into the watery depths.

At that moment, Edwin heard the clip-clop of horses' hooves in the yard. He ripped off the rope and raced through to meet the vanguard of Kinmer's posse as they dismounted.

"Be careful of the mud. It's really dangerous back there. But if you come quickly, you'll be able to get him before he falls in the well!"

The soldiers followed Edwin into the garden and their leader quickly took in the situation.

He directed a couple of his men to hold their spears out for Stan to grab on to and little by little, with much grunting and groaning, he was dragged out of the mud to safety.

By the end of the rescue the soldiers had nearly as much mud on them as Stan.

Edwin was glad to see what a totally foul, bedraggled mess Stan looked as his captors bound him and tied him to the saddle of one of their horses and disarmed him.

Kinmer, meanwhile, had dismounted in the yard and came rushing through to the garden. He caught Edith and Robert up in his arms and crushed them to him, speechless with relief and joy.

Granny came over to join Edwin by the cow shed.

"Don't you think it ironic, Edwin, that Saxons and Normans all look exactly alike under a coating of mud?"

# CHAPTER 25

An older man, who must have brought up the rear of Kinmer's convoy, hurried through into the garden after everyone else. He could only be Edith's father. The likeness was clear. The moment he saw Edith he was down on his knees beside her, gathering up both young parents and their child into an emotional bear's hug.

"They'll be all right now. Come on, Edwin. We have a few other things to attend to."

They went through to the yard where the rest of the little troop was gathered.

"These oxen have brought us all the way from Nottingham and I'm sure they'd appreciate a drink. Do any of you know how to take off their harness and feed them?"

"No problem, lady!" Two of the men stepped forward and began removing the yoke from Flower and Sunshine. They tipped the cart up on its end in the corner of the yard and led the oxen through to their stables.

"I don't know how we're going to draw fresh water for them with the ground in this state."

"Can't we put some straw down to soak up the mud?"

More helpers were called and between them they set to work to put the garden back into some semblance of order.

One of the soldiers cut half a dozen green branches from one of the shrubs. He stripped off the leaves and wove the stems loosely together into a large mat, to make a simple cover for the top of the well and make sure no more mud spilled down into the water.

A thick bed of straw was forked over the worst of the mud and trampled down so that it was not slippery. The buckets were retrieved from where Edwin had kicked them and refilled.

By that time, Kinmer and Edith were preparing to take their son home. Edith's father came to Gran to thank her and tell her that the family was about to leave.

Edwin and Gran walked through to the yard to see them off. Edith was seated on Kinmer's horse with Robert. Kinmer was standing at the horse's head, ready to lead them away. He stepped forward and spoke ringingly so that everyone could hear.

"We are forever in your debt. I, and my family, will live beholden to you for the rest of our days. You are my true followers. You wear the sign of the one-winged bird. You risked your lives to save my wife and child. Tell me what I can do to begin to repay you."

Before Gran could put a restraining hand on his arm, Edwin stepped forward.

"We don't have anywhere to live. Now this cottage is empty, can we stay here, please?"

"You shall have it for the length of both your lives, and that of all your descendents. I gift it to you, from my estate. It is yours, and with it, I hope, will go joy and blessings.

Edwin and Granny both bowed their heads.

"Thank you, my lord."

Lord Kinmer, in turn, bowed his head to them.

"Our home is very nearby. We shall be neighbours. We will see you soon."

Then he took the horse's bridle and led the way out of the yard, with his mounted followers making a guard of honour behind him.

Gran and Edwin stood at the gate and watched them go, the horses' hooves kicking up a flurry of dust from the road.

Then they turned and made their way back into the cottage.

"So, Edwin. We live to fight another day. Go and see if there are any charcoal embers still burning in the holder, will you please."

There were enough to rekindle the fire. Granny put on a pan of water to heat.

"What I'd really appreciate now is a nice cup of tea, but I know I shall be disappointed in that respect. Let's see what Garth and Arnie kept in their cupboards. If we're lucky, there might be some roasted acorns."

"What do you want those for?"

"Never had acorn coffee? When I was in the army, and coffee was in short supply, we often used to make do with roasted acorns. Not the perfect substitute, but better than nothing. And caffeine-free, of course."

They were in luck. When they found the acorns, Gran set Edwin to crushing them between two large stones, while the water boiled and she went to the stable to milk the cow again.

"Decaf acorn brew, coming up, Gran!" Edwin gave a flourish as he served them each with a steaming mug. "I found some more oat cakes in the cupboard, too."

Gran had picked a couple of apples on her way back from the cow shed.

"I think this amounts to lunch, don't you Edwin?"

"Is it lunchtime, then?"

"My stomach says it is. There's really no other way of telling, is there?"

"No. They're a bit short on clocks. They've got a funny calendar too. Lord Peverell was on about the date at my trial. I couldn't understand what he was saying."

"I think we both got through our trials pretty well, considering."

Edwin laughed.

"What, even though you were sentenced to death?"

"Well, yes, there was that. But he didn't actually know who he was sentencing, did he?"

"That's right! That was brilliant, telling them you were Amelia Bloomer. I thought that was great. When it was my turn, I said my name was Bloomer, too."

"Why did you do that?"

"Well . . . I wanted my name to be the same as yours."

"Is that so? Do you know what my name is?"

"Its . . . its . . . well, I just call you Gran."

"I know. But you don't think I was called Gran when I was your age, do you?

"No. Of course not."

There was a pause.

"What is your name, then, Gran?"

"My name is Edwina."

"What? Really? Like mine?"

"Actually, Edwin, I think it's the other way about. I think your Edwin is based on my Edwina."

"Do you mean . . . I'm named after you, Gran?"

"I doubt very much it's a co-incidence."

Edwin took his time to digest this new information.

"Gran?"

"Yes."

"I'm really glad . . ."

At that moment there was a resounding crash and somebody rushed past the window opening and across the garden. Edwin and Gran jumped to their feet and hurried outside. There was nobody to be seen.

"Who's there?"

"What do you want?"

They looked in all directions but there was no-one to be seen. Suddenly, without warning, a figure came running from behind the bushes and let out a piercing yell.

"You! You! I'll kill you!"

It was Bebba. She looked demented, her clothes in tatters, her hair flying, and a strange, wild look on her face.

She threw herself at Granny, who dodged to avoid her but was not quite quick enough to escape Bebba's frantic grasp at her arm.

"You gave my man up to the soldiers! I will kill you for that!"

"Bebba! Bebba! Calm yourself. This is no good for you, or your baby."

But it was hopeless. In her frenzy, Bebba was not listening. She started trying to beat at Granny with her fists.

Edwin rushed forward and grabbed Bebba from behind, dragging her off.

"Leave her alone! She's an old lady! You'll hurt her!"

"I'll hurt her! I'll kill her!"

Bebba dragged herself free of Edwin and turned for another attack. Granny tried to distract her by talking to her.

"How did you get here Bebba? They locked you up. How did you get out of the cave?"

"Huh! I know my way around those caves better than any of the soldiers. I grew up in that part of the city. We played in those caves as children, before ever the castle was built there. I always knew I could get away from there whenever I wanted."

"How did you get here?"

"How do you think? I've got two feet, haven't I?"

"It's a long way to walk. You should take better care of yourself. You baby's almost due."

"Don't you tell me what to do. I came here looking for my man. He would take care of me. And what do I find? The soldiers have him roped and bound and will take him to hang, while you sit in this house like you own the place"

"Well, actually . . ."

Bebba threw herself on Granny. She took her by the shoulders and swung her round and shook her as hard as she could. Granny's hair came down from its neat bun and trailed round her shoulders.

Edwin had never seen anyone so demented as Bebba. He dived at her, screaming, and tried with all his might to drag her away. But in her fury Bebba seemed to have the strength of six women. She ignored Edwin's desperate efforts to break her hold and carried on shaking until Granny went limp in her hands. Then Bebba took her hands from Granny's shoulders and Granny dropped to the ground.

"No!"

Edwin let go of Bebba and flung himself down beside Granny. Her eyes were closed but the eyelids were fluttering. He patted her face, brushed back her hair, took hold of her hands and squeezed them. He tried anything he could to get some reaction from her, but Granny lay semi-conscious on the muddy ground, completely unresponsive.

"You . . . you monster!"

Hot tears were scalding Edwin's eyes. He wanted to go and smash Bebba's face in, but he couldn't get up and leave Granny's body lying there. He knelt beside her, clutching her hands in his, willing and willing her to wake up.

He heard Bebba moving behind him. He turned his head and looked up over his shoulder to see what she was doing.

She had a big stone in her hand and her arm was swinging. The last thing Edwin saw was the stone getting closer and closer to his face. Then everything went black as the muddy ground came up to meet him.

## CHAPTER 26

When Edwin woke up there was a golden glow of late sunshine in the room. The curtains were pulled together but still one radiant beam slipped in between them and lit up the simple painted chest of drawers.

Mum was sitting on the hard little chair beside his bed. As soon as he stirred, she leaned forward and put a cold compress on his forehead.

"You feeling better, Edwin?"

"Mmmmm. I'm all right, Mum."

What was he doing in bed, in Gran's spare bedroom, at tea time? Why was his mother fussing over him like he was ill, or something? What was going on? Suddenly a terrible recollection hit him.

"Gran . . ?"

He struggled to sit up. His mother gently, but firmly, pushed him back on to the pillows again.

"It's all right, Edwin. You don't have to worry. Everything's under control . . ."

"No, it isn't! It's Gran. She's dead!"

"No. She isn't. She's had a stroke. She's been taken to hospital. But we don't know, yet, exactly how things will turn out."

Edwin groaned. He knew.

"She's dead."

He didn't want to look at his mother. Didn't want to have to believe it. He couldn't share the terrible reality with anyone who hadn't been there when it happened.

His Mum dabbed at his forehead again.

"I'm guessing Granny felt poorly in the night and went outside for a breath of air and you followed her downstairs. You must have got dressed in a hurry because you had your tee shirt on inside out. It looks as if Granny must have had a stroke in the garden. I can only assume you slipped and banged your head as you tried to help her. It's terribly muddy out there for some reason.

"I found you both when I got back here this morning. I called an ambulance. I had to stay here with you, of course, but I phoned Nanna and she set off straight away to the hospital. So Granny's got her daughter with her. There's nothing for you to worry about."

"Granny's dead."

"No, she's not, although she's very poorly. But we hope she's going to be all right."

He turned his face away from his mother. Tears trickled down his nose. He sniffed and tried to rub his face on the pillow to brush the tears away.

"You go back to sleep, pet." Mum leaned over and tucked him in.

"No!" Edwin's head swam as he pulled himself up and kicked the covers off. He pushed his mother's hands away when she tried to restrain him and struggled to his feet.

"I want to go and see Granny."

"We'll go tomorrow, love."

"No! Now!"

"We're not going now, Edwin."

"Mum, I need to go now! This is important." He lurched across the room looking for his clothes.

"There's not much point us going now. Nanna's there."

"Ring her, Mum. Tell her we're coming."

"She'll have her mobile switched off. You have to switch them off inside the hospital."

"At least give it a try, Mum. Please."

As it happened, Nanna's phone was on. She was walking back to her car.

"She says she'll go back inside and wait for us at the main entrance and show us the way up to the ward."

"Thanks, Mum."

Edwin washed his face very carefully. He had a bump as big as an egg on his forehead. He put on the clean clothes Mum had got out for him and they set off.

On the way, Mum pointed out a flat, square, stone building that looked like the town hall.

"Edwin, look. That big building up there on the rock. That's Nottingham Castle."

"No, it isn't."

It certainly wasn't the Nottingham Castle Edwin knew.

How could he ever tell Mum about Lord Peverell or the archer shooting at the apple or the prison up in the turret or Lord Kinmer's room with the tapestries on the walls and the goblet of mead?

Nanna was waiting for them. He was glad he didn't have to try and find the way on his own. The corridors seemed miles long and the lifts were enormous.

Gran was in the first bed in a small ward. She looked tiny, lying in a hospital nightie against the crisp white pillows. Her bed was surrounded by computer screens and machinery.

Edwin walked straight up to the bed and stood close beside Gran. She lay still, her hands on the outside of the covers. Edwin knew what strong hands they were. He wished they didn't look so old and veined and knobbly. Gran's eyelids still fluttered slightly, as they had done when she first fell. Edwin supposed that was how they could tell she was still alive. But there was no other sign.

He stood in silence by Gran's bed for a long time, until at last he turned aside and let Mum lead him away.

Nanna suggested they call for a Chinese take-away on the way back to the cottage. They sat in the sitting room and ate their meal straight out of the foil cartons. Edwin nibbled at a few noodles but he wasn't really hungry.

"Come on. Eat up, love. It's your favourite sweet and sour prawns."

But Edwin had no appetite. He felt suddenly very sleepy.

"I'm going to bed, mum."

"All right, dear. Listen, it's Sunday tomorrow and you and I have to go home. Nanna's going to stay here so she can go and visit Granny every day."

"Can't I stay here with Nanna?"

"No you cannot. You're back at school on Tuesday. Yes, first day of the new term. Don't pull that face. You've been saying for the last fortnight you were bored with the holidays. And I've got to go to work on Monday. We'll call at the hospital before we set off down the motorway. Off you go to bed now. Night-night. I hope you feel better in the morning."

Next day at the hospital Edwin hung back as Mum and Nanna each settled themselves in a chair at either side of Granny's bed.

A nurse was looking at the readings on the machines and making notes on a clip-board.

Edwin stepped forward. His mother looked round with an anxious little murmur as he spoke to the nurse.

"What exactly is a stroke? Can you tell me what's happened to my Gran?"

The nurse was an older lady, quite big and plump with a silly little bit of a paper cap fastened to her hair with a lot of hair grips. Edwin caught sight of her watch, pinned to her very large chest. It was upside-down.

"A stroke happens when there is a temporary loss of blood supply to the brain. It all depends how severe the blood loss is, and for how long. Some patients make a full recovery. Others are not so fortunate. It takes time to know what the outcome may be. In your Gran's case, we just have to wait and see."

"Thank you."

The nurse took Edwin's arm and guided him gently away from the bed. She kept her voice low so that no-one else could hear.

"You're very fond of your Gran, aren't you?"

"Yes."

"And she of you, I dare say?"

Edwin nodded. He couldn't trust himself to speak.

The nurse smiled.

"I saw the way you looked at her last night. There was such a lot of love in your eyes. If your Gran comes back from this stroke, you know, she will come back for you."

Edwin could feel tears prickling at the edges of his eyes.

"Live to fight another day?"

"Is that something your Gran said?"

Edwin nodded again.

"It's a good saying."

There was a pause.

"And if she doesn't come back?"

"Then you have to accept that it was her time to leave, and let her go."

The nurse patted Edwin on the shoulder. She stood close by him for a moment and then moved on to deal with her next patient.

Edwin desperately didn't want anyone to speak to him. He went out of the ward and stood in the corridor.

There was a notice board with details about local bus routes and a poster for a charity garden fete that had happened last week. He stood staring at the board until the big black letters telling him to wash his hands now were imprinted on the back of his eyeballs.

The ward doors swung open and Mum and Nanna came through.

"Come along, pet. We're going now."

They expected him to follow them away down the corridor but he couldn't. His feet wouldn't take him that way.

He turned back to the ward and slipped through the doors. He sat down in the chair Mum had been sitting in. He leaned across and touched Gran's hand. He felt awkward and clumsy. He was too far away from her. He got up and sat on the edge of the bed. That was better.

He took hold of both Gran's hands, squeezing them a little. They were warm and relaxed and rested lightly in his own hands.

"Granny. It's me. Edwin. The others have gone, only I came back because I wanted to say . . . I wanted to say . . ."

He bent over and kissed her very gently on the cheek.

He caught up with Mum and Nanna while they were waiting for the lift.

Bombing down the motorway in Mum's car, Edwin sat in silence. There was nothing more he and Mum could do but wait to hear from Nanna.

As they turned on to the M3, Mum made a suggestion:

"This trip was supposed to round off the summer holidays but it's turned out to be a bit of a nightmare. We'll make up for it at half-term. I'll take you to the Isle of Wight for a couple of days. You always like going on the ferry . . ."

"I don't want to go to the Isle of Wight. I want to go back to Kinmers Lea."

"Pet, Granny might not be there . . ."

"That doesn't matter. I still want to go back there."

"It seems a bit of a funny choice to me."

"That's the only place I want to go."

"Trust you to be difficult."

"Please, mum. Promise that's what we'll do. Otherwise I don't want to go anywhere."

"Well, all right. If you're so set on it."

"Thanks."

Edwin sat back in his seat and thought about Granny.

From the start, she had urged him to think for himself, she had set him tasks, taught him about making judgements, shown she trusted him. She had challenged him and so Edwin had challenged himself, and found he could cope.

And now, he knew he would cope with anything the world could throw at him. She had given him the strength he needed.

In his heart he didn't think Granny would get better and go home. Something told him it was her time to leave.

If he was right, Edwin had no doubt at all where he would feel closest to her. The best place to remember Gran was in the garden of the cottage at Kinmers Lea.